ADVANCE PRAISE FOR *TOUGHER THAN THE REST*

"*Tougher Than the Rest* is funny and dark in all the right places. It's everything that I enjoy in a short story collection: a not-too-distant future, intricate characters that are endearing and vexing, a struggle with dominating technologies, and a compelling look at community relationships and human responsibilities. Del Bucchia's sharp wit and keen attention to detail create utterly engrossing prose. These astute stories are thoroughly unique and entertaining, and I hope she explores more of this fascinating world she's generated in future books." **—Waubgeshig Rice, author of *Moon of the Crusted Snow* and *Moon of the Turning Leaves***

"No one is writing about class and wealth disparity like Del Bucchia, and *Tougher Than the Rest* reads like a guide for navigating the absurdity and ruthlessness of late-stage capitalism while still hanging on to your humanity. In these stories, characters search for real connection in a world where technology and corporate greed try to keep everyone isolated from one another, and the result is a collection that will make you simultaneously want to call your best friend and also dust off the guillotine. Del Bucchia's writing is wry without being cynical, dark without being despairing, funny without being glib, and above all, honest without spiralling into hopelessness. The horrors persist, but as Del Bucchia reminds us, so do we." **—Amy Jones, author of *We're All in This Together* and *Pebble & Dove***

"*Tougher Than the Rest* is a collection of stories that build like stacking blocks and connect like a web, with sharp prose equally humorous and dark. Grief hums beneath the surface of every story; characters grieve people lost to death or circumstance, the ballooning climate crisis, and lives made unlivable by late-stage capitalism. These same characters are forever reaching for connection and often find it in other women, friendships, and girlhood. You won't be able to put this one down." **—Jessica Johns, author of *Bad Cree***

"*Tougher Than the Rest* is a tender collection of stories that explore Vancouver of the near future. Del Bucchia's prose is wry, captivating, and cutting, as we spend time with lonely workers and outcasts trying to keep on keeping on in a world that values developers, celebrity, and wealth above all else. A moving, entertaining read." **—Zoe Whittall, author of *No Credit River***

TOUGHER THAN THE REST

stories

DINA DEL BUCCHIA

ARSENAL PULP PRESS
VANCOUVER

ARSENAL PULP PRESS
Suite 202 – 211 East Georgia St.
Vancouver, BC V6A 1Z6
Canada
arsenalpulp.com

The publisher gratefully acknowledges the support of the Canada Council for the Arts and the British Columbia Arts Council for its publishing program and the Government of Canada and the Government of British Columbia (through the Book Publishing Tax Credit Program) for its publishing activities.

Arsenal Pulp Press acknowledges the xʷməθkʷəy̓əm (Musqueam), Sḵwx̱wú7mesh (Squamish), and səlilwətaɬ (Tsleil-Waututh) Nations, custodians of the traditional, ancestral, and unceded territories where our office is located. We pay respect to their histories, traditions, and continuous living cultures and commit to accountability, respectful relations, and friendship.

Arsenal Pulp Press is committed to reducing the consumption of non-renewable resources in the making of our books wherever possible. We make every effort to use materials that support a sustainable future. This book is printed on paper made with 100 percent sustainable recycled fibre content.

"I Want Candy" was previously published in *Devouring Tomorrow: Fiction from the Future of Food*, edited by Jeff Dupuis and A.G. Pasquella (Dundurn Press, 2025).

EU Safety Regulations authorized representative: Easy Access System Europe, Mustamäe tee 50, 10621 Tallinn, Estonia, gpsr.requests@easproject.com.

Cover and text design by Jazmin Welch
Cover art by Jazmin Welch
Edited by Catharine Chen
Proofread by Alison Strobel

Printed and bound in Canada

Library and Archives Canada Cataloguing in Publication:
Title: Tougher than the rest : stories / Dina Del Bucchia.
Other titles: Tougher than the rest (Compilation)
Names: Del Bucchia, Dina, 1979– author.
Identifiers: Canadiana (print) 20260129941 | Canadiana (ebook) 20260134554 |
ISBN 9781834050461 (softcover) | ISBN 9781834050478 (EPUB)
Subjects: LCGFT: Short stories.
Classification: LCC PS8607.E482538 T68 2026 | DDC C813/.6—dc23

This book is dedicated to my beloved friends,
who are everything and deserve everything

CONTENTS

Wearing a hand-me-down grey MEC jacket, she catches the first train into the city. Hood up, hands in pockets, backpack strapped tight, Dollarama wireless headphones spilling music into her ears. The train passes buildings that have sprung up like mushrooms in the rain, concrete towers the colour of shaggy manes, matching her outerwear. Shorter buildings squatting over chain stores, vape shops, B_{12} injection bars. Entire blocks that look like they're made of windows. Everyone is looking in or out in a world-class city. Trademark Olympics 2010. Across the train car, people in business casual check their phones or gaze out the window at the darkness. Inside her jacket pocket, she holds her phone, doesn't take it out. Feels warmth radiating along her palm and her fingers.

NIGHT MOVES

I'm sorting through a bin of bras in the last Salvation Army in the city. If they were new, most of them would cost $300 each. Anyone who donates their barely worn support garments is wealthy, and to them, this is nothing. And with so few places to donate used goods, this old Sally Ann is filled with mid-luxury treasures. I tell myself it's sexy to be cheap. Saving money in this city is tough, but finding alluring panties at a reasonable price is maybe harder.

Standards for dating feel so high now. Can't send a successful sext without looking at least a little like you have half a career as an influencer who knows angles, lighting, and photo-editing apps, and some good underwear can go a long way to helping you look good. Especially when you're twenty-five years out from twenty. With the scanning software, everyone can tell how much you paid for anything. That's why the city has emptied of almost anyone who isn't wealthy. Oh, the pressure to be alive and visible.

So many people have moved out to the suburbs or farther, into the Interior. I'm surprised at myself. That I can still live here when almost every modest apartment rental has been knocked to the ground and rebuilt as luxury condos with mandatory work parties to continually improve their appearance. I'm lucky. To live in a small bachelor suite in a small building owned by an old couple who have somehow managed not to sell to developers. They're stubborn and admirable, and once they die my life might end, but for now I'm stable. I can work as an underpaid receptionist at a dental clinic and still not have to bus or SkyTrain for three hours to get to and from work. I'm a unicorn.

I select four bras. Two lace—one red, one black—a hot-pink bralette, and a smooth, silky strapless that still has a tag attached. They're priced too high for second-hand at a store operated by God-fearing, Jesus-humping, hateful, pious people, but I guess if the money goes to their church, then it's okay to charge thirty dollars for underwear someone else wore.

I'd hoped to get a robe too, but I'm being picky. I don't want it to be too faded, too pink, too Laura Ashley. Can't believe that came back around again. The cycle of style is an endless loop. And rich people can afford to participate every single time it circles back.

"Get out of there, both of you! That's not a toy."

A parent shouts at their two children rushing in and out of the crowded appliance area. The taller one, who's wearing a superhero shirt with fake muscles built into the chest and arms, has knocked over an ancient vacuum cleaner with his unwieldy chest. Small household items topple around it, a Jenga effect as they fall onto the floor. The shorter child gets caught in the vacuum cord but isn't troubled, just grabs the cord and swings it like a lasso at the superhero sibling.

The parent sighs and rushes over as their children collapse on the ground, laughing.

"I'm sorry. They just get so wild in here. There are always old things they want to look at. It's like a museum to them. Which they've been to, and they misbehave there too. I just wanted to get them some new shoes!"

I must have been staring, smiling a little at their rambunctious behaviour. The only housing co-op left in the city is four blocks away. This family is lucky too, I guess.

"It's okay, they're just having fun. And buying shoes is not that fun when you're a kid."

I leave my basket of underwear on the carpeted floor and help to right the things that have fallen. The tall kid rushes over and grabs the red bra from my basket to use as a mask. It does match the costume.

I lean the vacuum against what looks like a mannequin. A very tall, very buff, very shirtless, very realistic mannequin. Abs of steel on this mannequin. Very tight boxer briefs on this mannequin. Maybe it was used in a storefront to showcase underwear. The mannequin turns to me and says, "Hello, you look very sexy today."

I drop everything I've collected and squeak. A noise I'm sure my body has never made before. I look around to see if anyone else has heard, if anyone else is paying attention, if the mannequin really talked or I'm just that fucking lonely. The parent is again chasing down the children near the glassware, a site likely to see more collateral damage than these old appliances.

"I said, you look very sexy today," the mannequin repeats.

"Thank you?"

I walk around to the other side of the display to get closer to this mannequin that gives compliments. I see it's not made of plastic but silicone, fleshy and just a little pliable. I see a mark on the neck with text that reads "PLEAZER PRINCE PLEASURE ANDROID™." A robot. A sex robot? I poke its hard flesh near the spine. Nothing happens. I grab a bicep. Nothing happens. I go back around to the front and it says, "No, thank *you*. Your touch is very pleasant."

I reach for the front of the boxer briefs, my hand hovering near the flat area that I assume becomes a stiff one.

"Can I help you?" An older saleswoman is walking over, arms crossed in front of her chest.

"Oh, hi. I was just curious," I say, bending down to pick up my basket of clothes.

"Yes, we've had a lot of curiosity about this one."

"I'm sure you have."

"Well, we call him Mattel. Because he looks like a Ken doll."

His face has the mouth-deadness of a Barbie, but there is a little sparkle in the eye. Mattel. Why not just call him Ken or Barbie or Barb? Or Midge?

"What a unique name."

"Can I help you with anything?"

"No, I'm just going to buy these things and go. It's been a long week."

"Mattel is for sale, you know. We've only had him a few days, and don't think he'll stick around long."

I thank the employee and head to the cashier, stopping on the way to touch a few scarves and a large necklace in the shape of a panda chewing on a piece of bamboo.

As I pay for my second-hand items, all I can think is that of course some rich person is already tired of their beautiful sex robot.

Platinum Corp Development!
Fifty luxury condos in the heart of the city! In the sky!
Views of other luxury condos guaranteed!

The sign's been out in front of the Sally Ann for months. Getting rid of an affordable store to put up something else: development. Every week someone sprays graffiti on the sign, something new, something harsh, something cool. Today it says, "EAT A DEVELOPER, SAVE A SOUL." Then the real estate developers get a new sign, and then the graffiti reappears, over and over again. They have so much money, and those signs don't come cheap, with their thick, sturdy wooden posts and colour printing.

Under the photograph of the looming, yet-to-be-built residential tower, someone has written, "Help us. We feel so alone," in small Sharpie letters.

When I get home, I google makes and models of sex robots. There are so many now, though they've already fallen a bit out of favour. The trends continue to wax and wane. Robotics has refocused on work tasks: Walmart greeters, door attendants, receptionists. Hardly anyone has human receptionists anymore, except for more intense office environments. They need someone who can react to delicate situations, especially when something like dental hygiene is involved. Children crying and frantic parents and people coming out of anaesthesia require more nuance than robots can muster. At least emotional labour is still something my workplace can pay for. This has worked out for me, but who knows when that will change.

Still, the dental office I work at is full of robots and the people who care for them with delicate instruments. The flossing robot. The X-ray robot. The hygienist robot. The hygienist robot technician is very cute, a bit younger than me, and doesn't talk much. I don't even know his name. He moves in and out of the exam rooms at a rapid pace, checking on things, restarting the hygienist robot. Unlike Mattel, the hygienist robot doesn't have human-like skin or a sweet face. It's minimal—metal and motors. Not monstrous, but certainly not adorable.

The technician and I often take our breaks at the same time. Last week it was sunny for the first time in months, after the winter rains. Most of the dentists and the other receptionists don't like to go out in the sun. Cancer, they say. Yeah, we all know about cancer. There are so many cancers we could and probably will get. I've made it to middle age, so I accept it. The technician is one of the only other people who goes out on the roof. All we ever do is nod at each other from a distance. Maybe wave our lunches at each other to say, "Yes, I am eating and you are eating and we are both eating. We eat to live, and that is all we should acknowledge, because we know what happens after the eating. We do the natural biological function that follows."

On that first sunny day, we squished together in the elevator up to the rooftop picnic tables, along with another technician who was bringing equipment to an upper floor. The piece of equipment poked me in the thigh and I winced, making the smallest sound of discomfort I could. The hygienist technician looked over, concerned. I smiled and made a little face, a *yeah, that hurt, but I'm okay* face. When the other technician got off, rolling the equipment into the hallway, I clutched my thigh. No blood. Probably a bruise underneath my black thrift store pants.

"Are you okay? People should look at what they're doing," the hygienist technician said to me.

"Yeah, I'm okay. And yeah, there are other people out here in the world."

"So rude. I'm glad you're okay." He smiled at me.

Then the elevator doors opened onto the roof, and the bright sunlight caught me off guard. I reached into my bag to pull out my sunglasses, and when I looked up again, he was walking away to the far side of the roof. I went to my usual table alone. We didn't even nod or wave our lunches at each other.

It's been years since I've had a partner, a companion, a person, whatever you want to call it—just not *lover* because I'm too old and grumpy for that term. Who wants to be with a person who can't afford a fancy bed to fall into at night? Mattel. I would change that name. Something less reminiscent of a small pointy toy with painted-on hair.

I lie in bed, trying not to think about the hygienist robot technician or Mattel. But I can't stop thinking about both of them. I open my laptop and put on a cooking competition show so I can get angry at how annoying the chefs are and hopefully fall asleep because it's so boring.

Once Bridge left to go far east, to the farm towns, I knew I might not find a friend again. The days of potlucks and game nights and holiday get-togethers faded away. There aren't many people my age in the city anymore. Who's left? Like in a 1990s buddy comedy, do I become besties with a plucky child orphan? As if plucky orphans are abundant.

The first wave of departures from the city, from my circle, felt normal. Just people maturing, making changes. People tired of small apartments and able to buy bigger ones. People wanting more space. A whole big house. A dog. Kids. A deep freezer. Two deep freezers. A place to sit outside and get bitten by mosquitoes while surrounded by water features and sculptures and zoological topiaries. A third deep freezer.

Then housing became the best investment in town. In the country. And then some people just wanted a home of any kind. Space of any shape. Somewhere to rest after working their 3.5 jobs. Then other people wanted to own the most homes so they'd have money while other people had even less space.

Bridge had been my roommate for years. For a brief while, we managed to stay in our apartment together before we gave in and added another roommate, and then three, and then eight. Bridge loves her privacy, so even though she's now staying in a farmhouse with four other people, there is space, there are cows, there are places to hide from other humans. A forest. A river. We try to talk every night, but it can be so loud in the city that sometimes I just need to try and be calm before I sleep. Hold myself against the wall and find stillness. And then when I call, I get her voice mail. Staying connected in the modern age is supposed to be easy.

There are still students around, but most of them live in small huts near the university. The city runs on people who burn out serving coffees or steaks to people who have enough money to participate in diet culture. So many people I've loved have left that it's shocking this place is still so full of people. Young people, old people, rich people, even some former friends who classed out of our friendship. Tax brackets broke apart our quiz team and happy hour hangouts.

A year ago, I followed someone wearing a New Kids on the Block backpack all the way from one edge of the downtown peninsula into Chinatown. Too nervous to approach, I stayed far behind so as not to startle them. They wore dark denim cut off at the ankles and frayed, comfortable walking shoes, an oatmeal sweater, salt and pepper hair, and that backpack. Nostalgia threaded through canvas in neon colours, bright and hopeful. Only someone my age would care about the most mediocre popular boy band. A fiftieth anniversary reboot of *Spider-Man Loves Ant-Man* used NKOTB's first album as the soundtrack, and it was a huge hit. It was like catnip to me as a tween, and I had a crush on all those bygone boys. I tracked the backpack person through the darkness, past never-ending condo towers, through brief patches of light at select intersections, and down an alley between a few of the remaining buildings the real estate developer overlords hadn't yet turned to dust to favour their sturdy bank accounts. I watched them enter and leave a bakery, a bank, and then a small store that sold art supplies.

I picked up the pace as they approached a parklet populated with small concrete stools. There was actual pep in my step. They sat on a stool, their long hair covering their face as they set down their purchases on an adjacent stool. I slowed as I got closer, not wanting to scare them, to be a freaky stranger on the verge of screeching joyfully. But then they raised their head, and their face was too young, too fresh. Not a wrinkle to indicate the right level of worry in their eyes. An ironic high school student, headphones in ears.

No one notices me most of the time, so I cried openly as I walked back home, thinking about whether I could afford takeout or had to eat the leftover sushi rice in the beer fridge.

The next morning, I wake up and stare at my lonely toes poking out from the end of the quilt. To start things out right, I wash my face, put on my black low-cut tunic, and go straight to the Salvation Army a half-hour before it opens. A St. Patrick's Day display dominates the window: green shirts and shorts, plastic plants, and a large crocheted leprechaun holding a large crocheted pint of Guinness. It's too full of Irish spirit for me to be able to see whether the sex robot has been snatched up in the last fifteen hours. I tap my wrist—no watch there—impatient and anxious. Anticipating that someone has bought it, that I slept on it.

The older woman who always sweeps the front stairs unlocks the door a minute early and says hello. I thank her and walk through the New to Young Finds clothing aisle, straight to Appliances. The robot is still in the same place. Unmoved, untouched. I check the price. A lot, but still a deal. Hopefully, I have enough in my account to cover it. I don't have much credit left, and the banks are taking so much interest it scares me to use it unless it's an emergency. But maybe lacking a sex robot is a modern-day emergency. I'll have to eat dollar-store canned soup and ramen for weeks to make sure I can pay my rent on time.

I try to look him in the eyes, but the robot is facing away from me. I wrap my arms around his torso and firefighter-carry him to the till. The woman there continues to drop coins into the register, so I set the robot on the floor and drop my purse on the desk.

"I'll take this, please."

"All right, then. Now. This thing doesn't have a manual anymore, but you might be able to find it digitally archived. When it first came in, we thought it might be a cleaning robot. I remember those were all the rage for a hot minute. But this one is ... you know."

I nod. "Yeah, I know."

The cashier lifts the robot by the neck like he's a kitten. "Surprisingly light!"

"Oh yeah. I was worried about carrying it home."

"Yeah, you don't want to get on public transit with this thing. Enough creeps on there already, right?"

I tap my phone against the pay pad, stare down at it, wait for it to tell me the transaction is approved.

"Everyone here is gonna miss you, Mattel!" the cashier says to the robot. "You became such a mascot over the past week. Who are we gonna talk to while we're closing the till? Oh, I almost forgot," she says, addressing me. "Here's the charging station." She sets a large baby-blue plastic box with a handle onto the counter. It looks like a tool box.

I'm still clutching my phone, squeezing it so hard that it feels like my hand might form a permanent claw. Finally, the little pad beeps and says "approved" in a smooth British accent. I mouth the word *yes* and reach over to grab Mattel's hand.

"Looks like he's all yours," the cashier says, a wistful look in her eyes.

"I'm sorry," I say, forming a sympathetic frown. "Thank you."

She shakes her head, pulls a small receipt from the machine, and walks away without another word. I pull Mattel toward me and get him back into the firefighter's carry. When I reach the door, I realize I can't make it through while still holding him. I set him down on an old vinyl chair, prop open the door with a different vinyl chair, pick him up, and shuffle through.

At the bus stop, I stand him up next to me, as natural looking as a human companion waiting around like everyone else. His profile is sharp, his nose pointy in a way that's almost hazardous. Or pleasurable. I wonder if his hair will require maintenance, like a wig. I own a brush.

I can't even contemplate the rest of him yet. I didn't even consider care and maintenance.

It's gotten humid. I take off my canvas jacket and set it across Mattel's shoulders. The sun glows peach from behind the developer's sign, newly vandalized since yesterday. Now the graffiti reads "FUCK THIS FUTURE EMPTY LOT," and underneath, in Sharpie, "We have to help ourselves. Masturbate."

At home, I sit him up in my bed, staring at the small square window that doesn't even open for air. The women from the Sally Ann were right. Matty is a good name, a reasonable name, the name of everyone's boyfriend. And we've got all weekend to hang out, me and Matty.

I wake up with a start in the middle of the night. I can hear people rushing down the alley with shopping carts full of bottles and cans, but what wakes me up is someone screaming and throwing firecrackers at them from their condo window. They've paid good money not to have poor people scrambling to stay alive underneath their homes high up in the sky.

Lying on my side, I feel a pressure behind me, and it takes a moment holding my breath to realize I invited this into my bed. I don't remember if I put Matty's hand on my waist before I fell asleep or if he somehow knows to do this. I'm not sure I'll have total control over his programming, but the adjustments I made have got him speaking a little, which is the perfect amount.

"You startled me."

"How do you feel?"

"I feel okay. I was a bit scared for a second there. We can go back to sleep."

"Or we could not."

"You're really horny, Matty. I mean, I guess you're programmed that way."

Light from the alley is streaming in through the cracks in the old blinds. Matty's skin looks even fleshier in the dimness. I roll him over and myself onto him. His body barely moves, which unfortunately is like fucking a Teddy Ruxpin. But his penis vibrates and rotates, and he speaks.

"You're amazing. I love the way you do that. You feel so good. Oh god, yes. Please don't stop. You're the sexiest person I've ever been with. You smell of lavender fields. Your face is what I worship. Your body is a wonderland."

And then afterward, "Thank you. Do you need anything else?"

I don't need anything else. And it's not as if he could get up and make me a grilled cheese—but still, a generous offer. I don't have to clean up any man stuff. I just tell him I'm finished so he can reset.

"Good night, Matty."

"Good night, sexy."

I fall asleep facing the alley lights, Matty's stiff doll-like arm resting on my body again.

I spend my time at work allaying dental fears, booking upsetting appointments, and combing through message boards, searching for new information on Matty. After the first night, I discover that he's programmed to stiffen up at the same time every day. It takes a week of tweaking to get him to stop waking me up at three in the morning and instead enter a mode selected by me only when I'm interested and ready. "Sexy" seems to be his only form of address. I can't reprogram that, no matter how many buttons I press on his chest panel, how many times I restart him after inputting the correct key code.

I've learned a lot, and yet there are always new things to discover. There are special lubes for sex robots and expensive cleaning products you can buy. But also, there are tricks and hacks. If only they'd encouraged girls to go into STEM programs when I was a kid, I might actually be good at programming Matty. Or have a job that pays better.

At night I come home, sit him at the two-person table, and tell him everything about my day. He stares into my eyes in that way I like that makes me never want to stop talking. Then I shower, dress us both in matching pyjamas, and we watch an hour of TV. At 10 p.m., I switch Matty to sex mode and delicately remove our clothes.

In the morning I fold our pyjamas, set them under our pillows, kiss Matty, who stays in bed all day, and head to work.

One night Matty wakes me up, talking. It's like he's stuck, not physically but verbally. He keeps asking me, "How do you feel? How do you feel? How do you feel?"

"Matty, I feel great. How are you?"

But he can't stop, just repeats it over and over. I try to sleep through it, but I can't stop thinking about how I feel. I shut him down. I toss and turn. In the morning I scour the message boards, the manual, but none of the fixes work.

When I get to work, I consider asking the lunch-waving hygienist technician for robot tech recommendations, but I don't want to explain why or how a poor sap like me has a luxury sex robot, let alone an issue with the sex robot that I can't fix.

I keep Matty in bed, but turned off. He doesn't ask me how I'm feeling or tell me I look as beautiful as a summer sunset or that I'm very sexy today and he appreciates me. I curl around his solid, unmoving body and rest my cheek on his chest. I'm too scared to try anything in case I break this delicate machine. All through the night, I wake up crying, like I'm a teen again and can't manage my feelings, like this is a breakup I'll never recover from.

Finally, after two weeks, I decide to give it another shot. When I start him back up, nothing happens. I go to make some coffee, pour oat milk into my cup. When I get back to the bedroom, he is asking how I feel again, so I just say, "I'm horny, Matty," and lay him out. He continues asking how I feel the whole time, but I start to get into a rhythm. After I come and tell him I'm finished, he stops talking.

"How are you feeling, Matty? Oh my god, that was scary."

But he says nothing.

"Matty, what am I going to do with you?"

He turns in bed to look at me, both our heads—one human, one not—resting on pillows. He looks so vulnerable, too calm after such a strange ordeal.

"Whatever you want, sexy."

"I want to not feel like this," I say.

"How do you feel? How do you feel? How do you feel?"

The next night, after my shower, I shut Matty down again. I don't turn on the TV, just sit in silence.

It's been three months since I last heard from Bridge, and I need to hear her voice. I try her number. It rings and rings and rings. I leave a voice mail.

"Hi Bridge! I miss you so much. I hope life is treating you well. I've got this relationship or whatever it is, and I'm not really sure it's gonna work out. It's very one-sided. I just don't know. Anyway. Give me a call when you can. We should plan a visit or something. Not that I can afford to travel, but I'd love to see you. It would be good to get out of the city. I love you. I miss you."

Up on the roof, the sky is cloaked in a haze. In a few months, it'll be dark when I take a break up here at 4 p.m. I took a late lunch to avoid a patient who always accuses me of scheduling her in the worst time slots. It's not my fault she doesn't have a flexible schedule. Trying to make things work for people is honestly one of the best parts of my job, and I feel bad when I can't.

Oddly, the technician is up here late as well. He waves a sub sandwich at me. I wave my salad in its ancient Tupperware container. I take a few more bites, look out at the city. If I were even one floor lower, I wouldn't be able to see the mountains—all the buildings are too tall. I finish the salad, put the empty container in my bag, and walk over to where the technician is sitting.

"Hey."

"Hi."

"It's weird that we're always up here but never talk."

"Yeah, guess so."

He takes a second sub sandwich out of a paper bag and bites down on what looks to be at least four types of deli meat.

"Why do you come up here?" I ask.

He puts his knee up on the bench, rests his elbow on his knee, and holds up his sandwich right by face, shakes it a few times. Then settles back and takes another bite, gestures with the sub at the whole city.

"Just wanna look at the changes. Plus, the lunchroom smells like compost."

"True."

He takes another bite and stares out, away from me. "Okay, well, I'm not much of a talker," he says.

I don't respond, just walk back to the elevator and take it down to the office.

"Listen, I just ..."

As usual when he isn't asked a direct question, Matty says nothing. We're standing at the bus stop again. The first time he's been outside since the day I took him home. The bus is late, and I'm tapping my foot in an anxious rhythm.

He looks extremely cute. I bought him a navy peacoat and a sapphire scarf. He looks good in blue, so everything he's wearing is different shades of blue, including the jeans he came with. He's like a stock photo of an autumnal boyfriend.

"Have you been by the ocean yet? To the bay?"

"I'll go wherever you want me to, sexy."

"I want you to do a bunch of stuff you can't do. Like tell me what to do with my life."

I could turn him off for this. Just let him be the mannequin I'd first thought he was, but I can't do it. He keeps me calm when he's on, and it's nice to have him out in the world with me.

"How do you feel? How do you feel?"

His new default. I don't answer him.

When the bus comes, the driver barely notices as I tap two fare cards and shuffle Matty to a spot near the back. We pass places I used to go, places torn down and replaced by other places. The bookstore I used to browse at. The bar where we almost got in a fight because some woman swore Bridge was a regular on *The L Word: Dyke Redux*. I tell Matty about them as we move through this part of the city. I recount my life in small increments.

"That's where I lived with Bridge. She's the best. That place basically had silverfish instead of carpets. And there's the old bar we went to all the time. Well, now it's a juice bar, but still a bar. A different kind of bar."

As we move down the hill toward the ocean, the air has a hint of that salty sting. But everything smells different than it used to.

We get off the bus, me carrying Matty over my shoulder.

"How do you feel?"

"Matty, no."

We walk past families picnicking on the grass, teens vaping and tossing Frisbees on the beach. I move along the Seawall, knowing people are watching me, curious. We get to the small cove past the busy part of the beach. I flip Matty onto the old concrete wall, climb over, then pull him down after me. The tide is low. I have to walk out on the rocks. Luckily, there's no one here. It's too cool for most people to swim in this area, and it's not touristy enough to be an attraction. We can be alone, just like we always are.

I prop Matty in the sand, bend to tighten my bootlaces. I look up into his eyes and see that oddly lifelike energy pulsing through them. I stand back up and pose his arms outstretched so I can hug him tight, secure my arms around his body and whimper a little as I bury my face in his new-used coat. Smells like fake ocean, the cheapest cold-wash laundry detergent. I let go and wipe my eyes mostly dry. I place his arms around my neck and haul him up, cradled, and start walking.

The air is warm, the sky purple and dull. A heron swoops over the shoreline, a rare bird sighting these days. Across the bay I can see the tip of the dental office poking out, and to the left of it, a crane constructing another unlivable tower.

My feet hit the water. It's not as cold as I'd expected. I thought I would move in slowly, but once I'm in up to my ankles, I can't stop myself. I walk quickly, until Matty's body is almost touching the water. I squeeze his hand.

"How do you feel?"

"I feel sad, Matty."

A rush of wind catches me, encouraging me to keep going into the water. I walk in up to my knees. My jeans are soaked to my shins, waves lapping at my legs. Matty's legs dangle, his feet close to the water. As I move in deeper, Matty raises his legs, and his body feels heavier. His arms inch up over my shoulders, pulling him away from the waves. I get in up to my thighs and it's like he's climbing me. I'm so cold, and his bottom is now touching the water, waves brushing the back of his jeans. The jeans I dressed him in.

"How do you feel, Penny?"

I stop walking. "What?"

"Penny, how do you feel?"

I back up, turn around, and walk with my soaked and heavy legs, Matty in my arms, until I'm back on the beach. I sit him down against a large log.

"Penny, what are we gonna do today?"

"Matty, who is Penny?"

"You're Penny, sexy," he says.

I go to power him down but stop myself. I adjust his scarf, make sure he's secure in the sand.

"Penny, how do you feel? What are we gonna do today, Penny? Sexy, I am ready. Sexy. How do you feel?"

"Goodbye, Matty."

I turn and walk away. Matty doesn't turn his head, staring out at the water, at the other side of the city through the grey clouds. It's like I was never with him at all. When I get to the Seawall, I climb up the rocks and look back, and he's still looking out, not concerned in the least. I can still hear him talking.

"How do you feel?"

"I feel like shit, Matty," I say.

I sit on the rocks near the edge of the Seawall until Matty is submerged, his questions muffled by the high tide.

At Commercial–Broadway Station, she gets off the train to transfer to a different line. She checks her phone. 5:35 a.m. She missed the first one. But she'll be okay. None of her friends will be awake yet—it's too early, even for her jock friend who has practice at 6:15. The rink is a ten-minute drive away, and her friend gets up at 6 a.m. on the dot. The platform for the Millennium Line is empty on the westbound side. On the other side, people stand apart from each other, waiting to go east. They stare down at their phones. She discreetly takes a photo of them, figures under amber lights, tree branches casting shadows through the glass along the edge of the station. They look so normal. Unfazed. Their eastbound train arrives, and the platform empties. She takes a photo of the dark, empty space where they used to be and then puts away her phone.

TOUGHER THAN THE REST

"Tougher Than the Rest" Official Video

2.7M views

62,458 comments

@ToTheOne

I am 50 and have been divorced twice and lost my mom and sister and my aunt who was like a second mum. I finally found someone who makes me feel like we are both tough, survived to get to each other. This song makes me think about that and I can't stop listening to it.

@BigBossFan64

Wow. That's really incredible. I wish for something like this for me. I have had similar heartaches and griefs and still do not have answers for how to go on when things feel so lost. I am happy for you. This song is a favourite. Glad we can come together for music for a few minutes at a time. It's hard to not want to end everything when your life constantly feels like pain.

The power flashes out again. My laptop blinks off and on to tell me something is wrong, to try again. I refresh, but nothing happens. I shake the computer just a little, not enough to wreck it but enough to feel my frustration rattle the circuits. I need this thing to work in order to get paid, so I can't destroy it just because I have feelings about maybe not getting paid for work I can't do.

I've read this comment four times. Lots of people leave comments about the tragedy of their existence. But something about this Springsteen fan is so desperate. I need to see what BigBossFan64 is up to.

I'm tired, would love to sleep, but it's all freelance now at the agency I work at that EverEverStream uses to maintain their comments, so I need to stay up all night to get the job done. That's when the drunks are out, the porn spammers, the daredevils trying to post old recipes from *The Anarchist Cookbook* in the comments. I push my laptop off the pile of blankets I consider a desk and then use it as a flashlight to get to the breaker, which is beside my roommate's upper bunk; I'm in the lower one. It's a warm corner in a section of the open concept apartment we've carefully portioned. Our sleeping nook.

My roommate, Rory, isn't home yet from her actual leave-the-house night job. She serves at one of the bars that's open until 5 a.m. Once the city got rid of liquor and labour bylaws it wasn't No Fun City anymore. It was Work at All Hours Even More Than Ever Before City. I try not to crawl on all her stuff that's so carefully organized. Her childhood stuffed toy, Anti the Aardvark, takes up half the bed. He's like a boyfriend pillow but cuter and smells like facial moisturizer, the kind we get free samples of so we can stay moist on proper winter days. Anti is wearing a boa and a winter scarf. Ready for anything.

I flip the breaker off and on. Nothing. Building managers are the only people who aren't on call, can somehow manage a work-life balance, a weekend. Anyone who makes money off of housing when it's so precarious, expensive, and ridiculous sleeps well at night.

I hold my laptop up to the electrical panel to check if I'm doing something wrong. Nothing unusual. I go to the window in the bathroom. It faces down the alley. All I see is darkness. We're not the only ones—everyone's power is out.

I like this self-appointed night shift. There are fewer kids signing into their parents' accounts after school. I'm not assigned to a particular genre, but nights are when people watch nostalgia videos—a blast of youth after a few drinks or a different tactic to stay sober but still emotionally vulnerable when you want a few drinks. Ballads from the 1980s are my specialty, if scrolling through comments to find anything truly offensive is a specialty. I wasn't even alive when Springsteen was, of course, but somehow I get it. Bruce Springsteen alone is an emotional minefield for comments. Reading them makes me want to listen to the songs. Which I'm doing tonight, while working through the comments.

"Brilliant Disguise"
5.6M views
103,456 comments

@Rock4Peace
This song was a fabourite when I wuz a kid, bit now it has so much mor meaning because I have lived so much life and spent time away from people just because I couldn't cope with any more hurt,

but I am back now talking to folks and I feel like a lonely pilgrim, and Bruce really gets how relationships work.

"I'm On Fire (from Born in the U.S.A. Live: London 2013)"
12.1M views
303,239 comments

@deejaydoubleyou19664
Beautiful, haunting, peaceful, dramatic, all at the same time. Has other artist wrote so many classic songs?The sound the band got at an outdoor event was also brilliant. He ain't called the Boss for no reason!

Recently there was a lull in work for some reason. It lasted two weeks. A technical issue, they said, that made it impossible for freelancers to log in. On our secret freelancer Slack channel, we all talked about what might be up while we waited for more work, the kind that's usually never-ending. We speculated that they were changing policies, hiring people at a lower rate, changing privacy settings so they could spy on us. I missed reading the comments while I waited for new assignments, a little contract to activate me.

I could have gone out tonight but was too worried about money. Rory always gives me a few free drinks, at least. Once we got back to work this week, I had to catch up on those direct deposits I hadn't been getting. I logged in and it seemed nothing had changed, except the colour of the banner on the accounts page was blue instead of red.

I pack up my laptop and a blanket scarf, planning to look for a café within walking distance that has power. I make sure I've flipped the breaker switch back off and adjust the blankets and toys on Rory's bed so it looks like I haven't disrupted it. I lock the door. Check the lock. Unlock it and lock it again. Check the lock.

I walk through the alley and start over toward Coal Harbour. They have money there, and the power usually stays on even if it's out elsewhere. It's cold but not raining. At the intersection, there are a few guys obviously going out to party. They're passing a forty between them.

"Who wouldn't want to suck my dick?"

"Honestly? Do you want us to be honest?"

"Hey, you want a sip? You want to suck back from our bottle?" One of them thrusts the bottle in my face and I push it aside with a fist. Some alcohol spills out.

"Fuck. Bitch."

"Sorry, looks like you lost some!" I shout as I jaywalk across the street, just missing a Beamer that skids past. The dudes are too wobbly to chase me. This is why I never go out anymore. Only these kinds of dickheads can afford to party at the places I can afford to party, and I don't want to party with them.

The lights are on everywhere in Coal Harbour. I pick the coffee shop with the least light but where I'll still be able to see.

"Can I get an Americano, the largest size? And three chocolate-covered espresso beans, please."

The barista nods, looking tired, and shuffles over to the machine. There aren't many people here on a Saturday night, but this place is open twenty-four hours, and who knows how long the shifts are. My coffee appears. I smile at the barista as I tap my phone to pay.

"Thanks, have a good night."

"Oh yeah, thanks." Three little espresso beans drop from their silver scoop, clinking into an espresso cup that they hand to me.

I sit at a high-top in the corner and plug myself in, set up my laptop, and set my coffee far enough away that I won't elbow it onto the keyboard. I go straight back to where I left off, checking on BigBossFan64.

They've moved back in time to "The River," according to a comment posted three minutes ago.

> **@BigBossFan64**
> This song reminds me that we all make mistakes. And I've made so many that I don't know if I can even just stay alive. Don't even know if I want to.

Underneath, there are already five downvotes on his comment and a single reply that says, "Try TeenyMaxx for twenty-on days and ferl more alive, loved, and slimmer and more attrctive than ever. Click this link to renew your boody to its former glory."

Fuck, BigBossFan64 is getting roasted. I report and remove the weight-loss spam, then log in to the back end, upvote the comment, and send a direct message to my new late-night sad sack.

> **@CC880088** Hey! I've been following your unofficial Springsteen playlist all night. Sounds like you're struggling. I hope you stick around.

This was covered in the manual—don't respond privately to people—but this person needs a friend. I'm supposed to be looking for spam. Not to be confused with sponsored comments. Which are paid. Money straight to the corporation. Spam tries too hard. That's how you can tell. And there's always at least one typo. Sponsored comments are designed to look somewhat like a real comment, a story with feelings, but in the end it's trying to get you to buy a high-end weighted blanket or a motorcycle or diarrhea medicine. Spam needs to go because that's people sneaking their ads in; they haven't paid Big Video Platform to be allowed to spout off about insurance. I'd love to be paid to write that sponsored content. I know it like a second language by now.

I skip over to the next videos as they play through, dictated by the algorithm. A TeenyMaxx troll is in full force. In twenty minutes I catch a dozen more. Then I spend another hour filling out the follow-up reports for those.

I go back to check on BigBossFan64. Their posts today are so sad. And I see a lot of sad posts under a lot of videos for emotionally charged songs. Each user has a bank of comments that I have access to, in case they're doing something sinister like constantly posting ads. That's what people who want to make money off of ad revenue think is sinister. Then I can batch-report one account's entire bank and delete them. It's rare people complain about it, since most of them are bots or are people paid to target videos.

I go back through their bank history. They've been going hard on songs from 1988 for the past few weeks. Every song reminds them of something. A death in their family, a lost job, a breakup. But today's comments feel raw, like they're really going through some shit. A new comment pops in at the top of the bank feed.

Bobby McFerrin "Don't Worry, Be Happy"
16.2M views
11,444 comments

@BigBossFan64
I just don't know if I can keep on like this.This song has no fucking idea.

This is the kind of song I can't imagine someone searching for, but it's got 16 million views, and I shouldn't be surprised about what people want to watch. It's catchy. Bobby McFerrin deserved his success.

I keep scrolling through BigBossFan64's recent comments. Twenty new ones tonight. The Bobby McFerrin one was two minutes ago. No response to my reply yet. It looks unread.

My reported comment queue has grown to three hundred over the last twenty minutes. And I have to go through them all before morning. I open a separate tab and keep BigBossFan64's account open there while I work. It's marked as a watched account, so if they leave another comment, I'll be notified.

I scroll through the queue. Half the accounts are spam, likely run by the same company offering free gifts if people "CLICK THE LINK ♡." Batch-report and delete. Same with a Christian dating site. "Find your soulmate! I did. Use JesusMeetNGreet to find someon as pure of hart and body as you! You're soul will thank you."

It takes three hours to get through the abusive comments on an Ariana Grande video. Apparently, a bunch of people are piling on what seems to be a young girl who doesn't like people sexualizing the pop artist Zizi or historically fat-shaming Cass Elliot.

@cazimi22
She's a young woman. You might as well be sending her dick pics.

@cazimi22
Cass Elliot is a million times more talented and interesting than you'll ever be!

I hear a group of young women outside laughing. They're crowded around a Platinum Corp development billboard across the street. It's in the last vacant lot in the area, formerly a mediocre family restaurant. Not really worth saving, but more affordable and aesthetically pleasing than the asymmetrical glass condo that will crop up in its place.

I go back to scrolling, glancing over to see there is no new activity from BigBossFan64.

"Hey! Hey! Be careful! Don't do that!"

The barista has run out of the café and across the street, waving a dishtowel in the air. The Platinum Corp sign is now on fire. The girls are running away, toward the park. In all caps, graffiti on the flaming sign reads "DIE DEVELOPERS." I have enough time to take a photo and send it to Rory before the billboard is engulfed in flames, the message illegible.

The barista comes back inside, talking on her phone, probably with 911, but fire engines are already en route, their sirens screaming toward the harbour. Someone in the tall buildings above likely called as soon as the fire started. She finishes her call and hangs up, then uses the towel to wipe down the already-dry counter. The few customers are all leaving. I walk over to the bar amid the commotion.

"Can I get one more? Just a regular coffee. Whatever you've got." I hand her my stainless-steel mug.

"Sure." She sighs and flings the dishtowel onto the floor.

"Why did you run out there? Big fan of Platinum Corp?"

"No, I just didn't want anyone to get hurt. I dunno. I just reacted. I really don't know what I thought I was doing."

"It was impressive. I mean, even though Platinum Corp can fuck right off," I say.

"I'm with you. Those new condos make me think the designers never played with LEGO as a kid."

"Totally."

"I texted my boss a photo of the fire. No response. So I called and explained, and he says I can close since no one will be coming in while they shut down the street. But he won't pay me, so yay! I get to leave early. Sorry, I'm really going on. These night shifts mess with my brain."

"Don't apologize. I work night shifts too, but not in public."

She sighs again and goes to get the coffee. The tip jar has a note telling customers to "Fight for change, and then give it to us."

"Oh shit," I mutter.

"What?" She hands back my mug, now full of steaming coffee.

I rummage through my pockets and drop all the coins I have into the tip jar. "I'm sorry I didn't tip you earlier."

"It's okay. Most people are so bad at tipping."

Before I pack up everything a second time, I see a notification about BigBossFan64, but the barista is waiting to lock the door. I don't have time to check it now.

"Have a good night," I say, rushing outside.

On the street, the firefighters look annoyed that there are still people in this heavily populated area, that a twenty-four-hour café is open at night.

My phone lights up with a text from Rory.

Cal, please come down. I want to see someone I love because I'm so tired. I need you to give me life!

Can you get me some wifi? power was out at home?

Ugh. Fine. But you have to have some fun first. Be a fun girl for once!!!

Ugh. Fine.

Come to the alley and I'll leave the door propped open beside the dumpster.

The place is packed, and I feel myself sweating as I walk through the mess of people to get to the bar. There is a single seat at the end near the bathrooms. I cram all my shit onto it and stand to the side. Rory is being her best bartender self. Pouring up drinks quickly, but chatting to people with just enough charm for them to toss bills into her jar, hit the 25 percent tip button on the pay pad.

"Hey, Ro."

"I thought you might be an asshole and not show. But deep down I also knew you would."

"Thanks?"

I pull out my laptop and fire it up. It's got enough power for two more hours of report, review, delete. There are several notifications for BigBossFan64.

"Working already?" Rory says. "I have a nice hazy Pilsner here waiting to swim into this pretty, clean pint glass. We're women in our twenties in the twenty-first century Anthropocene. We have to have fun while we're working or we'll die of depression."

"Fine. True," I say.

A tall tipsy man throws himself at the bar. "Excuse me? Can I get a drink here?"

"Oh sorry, no, this is the Genius Bar!" Rory yells back, then to me: "'Kay, I'm gonna work for a bit. I'll drop off a beer for you."

"I'm fine!" I shout. I click the first notification, another comment.

"Handle with Care" The Traveling Wilburys

82.1M views

204,931 comments

@Marx Alvord1

Id imagine, isn't this a treat not unlike getting to watch Michelangelo, Leonardo, Botticelli, Rembrandt and John Singer Sargent all painting together ...

@BigBossFan64

They don't need the comparison because this is a masterpiece all its own. Orbison's voice and the lyrics on loneliness just splay me open. It's a hopeful song, but it destroys me. Sometimes hope hurts so much. Thinking something good will happen, but it never does.

I see that there's also a response to my DM. I click.

@BigBossFan64 Thank you.

Not as wordy as the rest of their work.

"Still working?" Rory slides over with my beer. I take a sip and smile at her, throw her a high-five.

"Thank you. I might need to go somewhere quieter. Is there a storage room or something?"

"Don't you want people to hit on you?"

"Not really."

"Oh."

"You know me. I already saw a literal fire tonight. That's hot enough for one evening for this ol' gal."

"I know, it's just, you seem like you want to talk to people when you do talk to people, but mostly you're at home not talking to people."

"Great analysis." We both laugh, and I take another sip. "I'll finish this one and see how I feel. The power going out fucked me up for work."

"I know, I get it. You want some chips? Don't answer!" Rory runs back to her post behind the bar and tosses a bag of salt and vinegar to me. We air high-five.

My direct message didn't do the trick. I'm not supposed to contact commenters on the back end. But sometimes I can't control myself. I got written up once and have behaved myself ever since. Until now. BigBossFan64 is still logged in.

@CC880088 Hi, I'm a Comment Custodian here at EverEverStream. How are you this evening?

@BigBossFan64 Hello?

@CC880088 I just wanted to check in on you this evening.

@BigBossFan64 Why?

@CC880088 I monitor comments on the site and someone reported one of yours as a concern.

@BigBossFan64 Oh no. I didn't want to upset or hurt anyone.

@CC880088 Not like that. More of a concern that you might hurt yourself.

More comment reports are rolling into my feed. I see them popping in one by one a tab over from our unsanctioned chat. Hundreds flooding in. Music is pulsing through the bar.

@BigBossFan64 That's very nice. Thank you. Or whoever reported that. I'm fine really.

@CC880088 From your posts, you don't seem totally fine. I mean, you seem nice and everything, like a fine person. Sorry.

@BigBossFan64 I understand. No need to apologize.

"Oh my god, is that person doing work at a bar? This place is really going downhill."

"I think she just yawned. In a bar. Like, take off your hoodie, have a shower, and put on some pants that fit, you know?"

"Ha ha ha ha ha!"

The high-heeled crew talking shit about me totters past to the mirrored sinks in the area outside the single-stall toilets. It must be nice to not work on Saturday night, to spend time with people you like.

@BigBossFan64 I didn't know you could send messages in here.

@CC880088 Only if you have access, like I do. You can't message another user or anything.

@BigBossFan64 Well, it's nice to meet you. Thank you again for reaching out. This is a good feature.

@CC880088 Yeah, I mean, I'm not supposed to do this. I could lose my job.

@BigBossFan64 Oh.

@CC880088 I was just concerned. I wanted to see if you were okay.

@BigBossFan64 Who's really okay?

@CC880088 Yeah. Good point.

@BigBossFan64 Honestly, I don't know if I'm even close to okay. I have to go.

@CC880088 I can see all your comments—you've really gone through some shit. And other people in the comments can see that too. I wish they would respond sometimes to give you support. Do you have people in your life to talk to? It can be hard to feel alone.

I check the other tab and go through a few comments as quickly as I can. Delete. Fine. Delete. Batch-report. Fine. Batch-report spam. Fucking Trooper.

Trooper "We're Here for a Good Time (Not a Long Time)"
35.1M views
31,003 comments

@MayDayMayDay
my step moms best friend past away due to cancer and this was played at her funeral a couple days ago

@KarenLoooooove
OMG this is beautiful it reminds of being a kid again 😭😢 when everything was just the way a kid should grow up I don't know if that makes sense 😁 and especially when my dad was alive. I lost him in 2032 when I was 10.This reminds me of enjoying Christmas all together.

Everyone's really feeling everything tonight. I should have checked to see if there's a full moon. Any planets in retrograde. It's definitely Pisces season. I click back into the conversation tab, but BigBossFan64 has logged out. I couldn't have been gone more than five minutes.

"Hey Cal, I wanna head out early. Viv is gonna finish the night with Jonah. And a bunch of customers left to go check out that bonfire damage."

"It wasn't really a bonfire. But I get it."

"'Kay, let's get! We can grab a pizza and get to bed before dawn for once."

I check again to see if BigBossFan64 is back, but no. My last question in our chat left unanswered. I leave one more before we head back home.

@CC880088 Please let me know you're okay.

We stop to get a cheap Freshslice, pesto and cheese. When we get home, the lights are still off in our building and all across the West End. And the emergency lights are already out too. I use what's left of my phone's power to shine the flashlight as we walk up the stairs. We climb into our beds with the pizza. Rory splits the cardboard box in two, divides the pizza, and hands half the box, filled with still-hot bread and cheese, down to me.

"So, I was messaging with someone tonight."

"Excuse me?"

"Not like that. I've been watching their account for weeks, and the messages have just started to get sadder and sadder, and tonight one really struck me as, like, suicidal or something."

"Oh, shit."

"I know it's not my job and I'm not a therapist or anything, but I dunno."

"I told you, you like talking to people."

"Shut up, I hate people."

"Keep telling yourself that."

I settle into a horizontal position, finish my last slice, and chuck the empty box half across the apartment like a Frisbee.

"Hey, I stepped on Anti earlier. It was in the dark, and I cleaned him up. Sorry."

"He forgives you."

Rory taps on the bunk frame with her foot. A little goodnight.

I wake twelve hours later. It'll be dark again soon. I flick the bedside lamp—we have power again. Rory is in the kitchen guzzling orange juice. She always smacks her lips when she drinks OJ.

I take a pee and by the time I'm done, Rory's gone off on a run. She loves to exert a little energy as soon as she wakes up. She's always wired after sleep. There's still a bit of juice left and enough milk and granola to make something of a breakfast in the late afternoon. I'd planned to take a day off, but I decide to quickly log in to see if there are any notices for BigBossFan64. I spoon cereal while I enter my password. But there's an error message. My password isn't accepted. I try again. Nothing. I check my email to see if I'm due to change it. Lots of notifications from work last night, and an email from my boss, from 9 a.m.

Dear Calliope,

There was some unauthorized activity detected from your account. We understand there are glitches and reasons for this, so for the next twelve hours your account is on lockdown while we investigate. Once the investigation determines whether or not this was a violation we will inform you of the results. If it was not a violation we will return your access at that time. You will need to change your password if you're granted access. Sorry for this inconvenience and work stoppage on any important accounts you were monitoring.

Best,

Ron Molloy
Comment Custodial Inc.

"Fucking shit." I spit cereal onto my keyboard.

I go into incognito mode and search EverEverStream for videos that BigBossFan64 might have commented on recently. Thinking he maybe went down a Traveling Wilbury's rabbit hole, I start with Bob Dylan and end with Jeff Lynne. I look for an hour, but nothing. I try every song on *Tunnel of Love*, including all the live versions. Nothing. Maybe their account is also locked. My uneaten cereal is a soggy mulch, but I don't feel like eating anything else.

I stash my laptop under my mattress, though if anyone broke in I'm sure they'd find it. If they even assumed we had anything worth stealing in this little nook. I grab my backpack and walk the same way I went last night. This time the sun is going down and it's pretty, no dudes yelling at me in the street. An old couple jaywalks across the street, holding each other's arms to stay steady. They stop at a bench on Barclay and sit together, like they're waiting for something else nice to happen or enjoying the nice thing that is happening. Squirrels natter at each other in the trees; they're waiting for spring too. For things to warm up. I forgot my toque, and there's a light wind blowing into my ears.

In Coal Harbour everything is normal, except the block across from the coffee shop is covered in police tape. Someone spray-painted "Nice Job!!" on the pavement in front of the burnt billboard. The barista from last night isn't in the coffee shop. It's full of people enjoying the golden hour. Chatting in groups. Working on screenplays and novels, practising their English, eating baked goods. I walk back home along the water, watching a proper sunset for the first time in forever. Geese have overtaken most of the grassy areas along the Seawall, but it's beautiful if you look out and above them, past their shit to the horizon, the mountains, the sea.

When I get home, Rory is taking a nap. I try to log in again, but it hasn't been twelve hours yet. So I settle in to watch some videos. A weird choice, but how else to kill time while I wait to get back to work?

The next morning, I get an email saying everything is fine. Nothing was found in the analysis, and I can get straight back to work tonight. I log in and my queue is as long as ever. Really cheap spam coming in hot.

> I can do graphic design work of any kond. Look a my digital card here.

Again with this guy.

I check my chat window, but it's been cleared of conversations. Nothing there. I look again for my new friend. I should be able to locate anyone I've looked into before, but BigBossFan64 isn't there. There's no report. No activity from them. In the comments, diet lollipops give people diarrhea like always, and anonymous sad people disappear from the internet without a trace. The usual.

When Rory comes home, I'm crying on the couch.

"What's wrong?"

"Just a bad night at work."

"Shit, and no one even tried to put a finger in your asshole while you were mixing Long Islands." I punch her shoulder lightly. "I'm kidding. The internet is a cesspool."

"I'm sorry people are such creepy fucking assholes, Rory."

"I'm sorry everyone is so fucking sad."

She goes to the fridge and gets a two-litre of orange soda, cracks it, and pours it into wineglasses.

"Cheers!"

"To us working assholes in our twenties."

Rory has convinced me lately to go on evening runs with her. I'm slow and I really just walk, but it's nice to get outside. As spring comes on, the brighter evenings give me more energy, and when I start work I don't immediately feel like I'm going to die. Instead it takes a few hours, like it might for a normal job.

We stop for street meat before heading home to shower and start our work nights. There are so many tourists that we have to wait twenty minutes for our hot dogs. We eat them ravenously as we walk up the hill.

"You've been running with me for a whole month now."

"Yeah, I guess so."

"It's nice to see you out."

"Is all this just so I don't stay inside all day and night?"

"Hey, I love you and just wanted you to get outside. So yes, that is why."

The power is surging in and out. I'm cold, but the heat was cranked before it went to shit, so it could be worse. Spring is not here yet. The late-April temperature has dropped to five degrees. Rory's napping, so I've got headphones on. Don't want her to hear my "granddad rock," as she calls it. I go through the first item on my nightly list. Not bad. Could be worse. Every time the power comes back on, I get another 10 percent charge to keep going.

I keep a second tab open to listen to songs and watch videos. I'm logged in on a private account, with my official custodial one in another browser. Under the video for "Thunder Road" I see a familiar writing style but a new name. I respond as myself.

@EStreetBaby

Someone once asked me if I was okay and I just said are any of us okay? I guess I was hoping you would all be okay. We've got the music. And that's okay.

@CalliopeNewMillennium
I was born just over 75 years after these songs came out but sometimes they get to me.

@EStreetBaby
Yeah, me too. Me too. Ya know.

@CalliopeNewMillennium
Have you ever listened to "Born to Run"?

@EStreetBaby
You've gotta be kidding me?

In one browser, I batch-report and block, batch-report and block, while in another browser, I listen to songs that mean something to someone, that are starting to mean a lot to me too. I listen to the guitar, the vocals, the clack of my keyboard. I imagine us being in the same room. We'd listen to songs in the dark, loud booms above us as my neighbours blast contrasting music. But we're just two people who don't know what each other looks like, talking about music on the internet while everyone else sneak in to try to sell us something we're not interested in.

This leg of the trip is short. She's the only one on the entire train. She puts her backpack on her lap and unzips it, checks to make sure everything she needs is inside. Inventory: four cans of spray paint, two pairs of gloves, a neatly folded stencil between two sheets of cardstock, and the large zippered pouch she uses as a wallet. Satisfied, she closes up the backpack and turns it vertical in her lap so she can barely see over the top. Her knees bounce up and down, her sneakers rising and falling underneath her. After a few minutes, she stands up, whips the bag onto her back, and waits by the door for the train to stop. The walk down the stairs is lit, but as soon as she gets to the bottom, it's dark. Gravel sounds under her feet as she shuffles to the street corner, eyes darting back and forth, hand on her keys in her pocket. A full minute ahead of the scheduled time, she stands and waits at the barely marked bus stop.

IT'S ALL OVER NOW, BABY BLUE

I don't wear gloves. With bare hands, I thrust the flimsy dollar-store toilet brush into the water over and over again, scrub with vigour. The water splashes onto my wrists, up my arms, sloshes onto the dress I bought on clearance at Old Navy to satisfy myself after cleaning up vomit a different time. Trying to purchase a feeling. I've always been an advocate of that. Though it never worked much for his chronic pain, depression, anxiety. Not in the long run. Which, it appears, was cut short. What if I'm not grateful every day for the time we spent together? What if I want to scream into the toilet bowl as I clean it of his vomit for maybe the last time?

Of course, Framebook is the thing that pisses me off. Couples and their self-congratulatory posts about cohabitating in legal matrimony for multiple years, as if all it takes is a self-congratulatory post once a year to have a functioning marriage. Really? Every day, every minute, every hour, they're grateful? What about when he ignores your request to engage in a healthy fight? When you just want some peace and quiet? When the bills start piling up and no one can bother to do anything about it except let them accumulate in a kind of sculpture on the subject of late capitalism and debt? When the way you're living feels like a scarf made of fire ants wrapping itself around your body? This morning, top of the feed: Ellie and John's wedding photo, shared On This Day every year since the memory-jogging feature within the app was invented. Their smiling faces against the backdrop of the very park where my own husband claims to have somehow ended his life and disposed of his own body.

The note left on the kitchen table was brief.

> Please don't look for me. I've gone into the park. They'll never find my body. Love you.

It was a surprise that he actually told me where he was going. Not that it was specific, but he was generally not that communicative these days. Those days. Whenever. Sending the briefest texts. He was silent most of the time, aside from his sighs. I started to think of them like his sitcom catchphrase. If our life was a sitcom, it was very modern. No laugh track, single camera, no quirky neighbour bounding in to break the tension. We were a cable comedy, with few laughs and viewers writing thoughtful think pieces about how not enough people were watching this barely comedic half-hour of human interaction.

The past few days have been blurry and bleary. Walking around our one-bedroom apartment, picking up objects without purpose, putting them down in different locations. A small ceramic owl moved from the coffee table to the nook by the door where we drop our keys. A book about the endangerment of whales that neither of us read now migrated to the ottoman. A tray of candles that I walked around with like a server balancing drinks, unsure of where they belonged, before finally placing them oddly at the side of the kitchen counter, blocking the microwave.

He's only been gone a week, wherever he is. I believe him. He is gone. Whether he's dead, I'm not so sure about. But his body isn't here and mine is, and somehow this little piece of his insides was clinging to the back of the toilet bowl lid. The last thing we ate together was a Domino's pizza. Both of us too tired to cook. Both of us fascinated by the live delivery tracking app.

After we ate, we sat on the couch and watched a documentary. A group of women in a small town were trying to convince the men that they were capable of running the drug trade. And they obviously were. He commented that one of them looked like his grade one teacher—she'd always seemed a bit tough, like maybe she made moonshine by night. She was pretty too, but everyone was scared of her.

"Just like you want people to think of you," he said to me.

It was his version of a compliment, the kind I appreciated. After he put on an action movie, I fell asleep with my head on a throw pillow in his lap. The bright visuals and fast pacing always tired me out.

But now I've scrubbed the regurgitated tomato sauce, cheese, and crust away, flushed it down with chemicals. Without his body—slim, sad, and somewhere else—I've flushed away his remains without ceremony. I almost feel tears coming on, but they stop. I take off my dress, wipe my face on it, and toss it into the laundry hamper where our clothes still mingle, flakes of his skin, his hair, and probably grosser things too still clinging to the fibres of the clothes I bought him.

"Can I please come back to work?"

My boss stares at me in disbelief. Post-note, no one thinks I'm in my right mind. But I haven't shaved off all my hair or gotten a commemorative tattoo in the middle of the night or had a screaming breakdown on the corner of Robson and Burrard. I'm not at my best, but I'm not acting unreasonably.

I've draped myself over a chair in her office. Upside down, Li looks less intimidating than she might otherwise. Above her is a cheaply framed photo of a basic beige teddy bear with an equally basic white bow propped on a darker-toned beige chair in the middle of a display of nut-brown wooden tables and bookshelves packed with books, their spines all beige. The colour palette is horribly bland, but it somehow speaks to my heart. We both need a pop of colour.

"Listen, how long has it been?"

I sit up and pick at the dead skin around my nails. "It feels like one second and a thousand years. Time is a flat circle. And that means I can do stuff whenever I feel like it. Including working."

Li sighs and busies herself rearranging papers on her desk. This is what she does whenever she's trying to figure out how to talk to someone asking for something unreasonable, like a three-week vacation during Christmas or a raise that's way beyond company protocol. I'm a petulant employee to her now.

"You know I think you're the best, and not having you here is the worst. And you know I'd rather be focused on Tinder matches than covering for my best manager. But you also know that you're grieving, right? You know that he's dead?"

"Well, is he really, though?'

She stops piling papers and pushes them to the side, opens her desk drawer, and takes out two bags from her stash of sour candies.

"I think you need more time."

"Time, time, time, that's all I hear! I just want everyone to fuck off with that shit."

"Hey! Come on."

I slouch as far down the stiff wooden chair as I can.

"Li, I'm sorry that you're missing out on hot lays because of me and my life. Sorry about that."

"Oh, I know. And I missing having you here so I can describe the various ways men have pumped my body into oblivion, in good ways and very mediocre ones. But it's too soon for you to come back."

"Do I still get my discount?"

Li nods and laughs, then unzips the bags of candy—colourful little humans lying on their backs and fronts. Delicious little sugary-sour bodies.

"It's not the 1960s, so I don't have a bar cart, but we have Sour Patch Kids."

I grab a handful. Now that I'm eating them, I realize I've hardly been eating at all. I'm starving, but the thought of eating anything other than these high-fructose corn syrup children nauseates me.

"Are there any prestige dramas anymore? I feel like they've fallen out of favour. It's all reality TV where someone almost dies or gets married seventeen times in one season. What's hot now, Li? I feel behind."

"Oh, I've got a few. I'll make a list. That's what you need, to stay home and binge something."

"We need a Sunday-night session, but without work stuff this time. If I ever clean my apartment, you can come over and show me some shows. I will order your favourite takeout. I will let you fall asleep on my big couch and call you a cab. I will go through your matches and respond to dudes for you. Tell me about Tinder."

She looks at me like I'm not ready to hear about Tinder.

"I might need to use it now, Li. And I'm really fucking unprepared."

"Goddamn, Nettie. Can you slow down for one second? One more week, at least. Then we'll talk again about work."

The spring sun blares down, and I pull out my sunglasses.

I'm a task-oriented person. I learned that from some kind of personality test I once took, and I know it because, left to my own devices, I can't quite figure out what to do with myself. I made a list this morning to get myself out of the house. "Talk to Li and try to go back to work" was at the top, and of course that did not go as planned.

The only other task was to go to the bank and deal with some financial stuff. Which sounds horrible, so I refuse to do it. Every time I walk past a bank, my throat dries up, and I immediately change direction and go wherever that takes me. A few blocks ago, I ended up in a loop, and to avoid getting caught in a Möbius strip of boredom, I jaywalked across a busy street.

I walk to the lagoon at the entrance to Stanley Park.

"Are you fucking in here somewhere?" I yell into a patch of tall grass. A duck crosses my path, and an older man does a double take. He thinks I'm talking to the mallard. I might as well be.

I circle the lagoon three times. Watch the water. Every ripple is a sign and nothing. I stop near the Nature House, then walk down closer to the water, where I'm not supposed to go. A duck lands on the surface.

"I haven't seen him."

I look around. The Nature House is closed, and there aren't any creeps jerking off above the walkway.

"Hey yeah, it's me. The duck. I'm a wood duck, actually."

I swivel back around and stare at it. "Excuse me?"

"I heard you. You've been muttering to yourself this whole time."

I probably have been. My husband always used to ask if I was talking to him or the universe. Sometimes it was both. I love to mutter. I love to talk. And I want for him to hear me, for the universe to hear me.

"No one's looking for him anymore," the duck continues.

I sit down on the narrow dirt path. "Hello? What … the … fuck."

The duck swims in a neat loop. Dusk is coming on and the light is golden and the sky pink, and it makes me want to drink a Slurpee. I stare at its little face, its feathers like perfectly applied makeup. We lock eyes, I think. I drop my head and look at my reflection in the muddy water, then grab a handful of dirt and throw it in to break up the image of my face. The duck eases away, seems to huff, and then swims as close to me as possible.

"No one is looking for him," I say. "Except for me. And I'm not even really doing that."

"Well, I haven't been looking, but I haven't seen anyone who wants to be lost or gone."

The duck comes up on shore, wings raised to shake them dry. I can't tell if I'm dizzy from not eating or from talking to this duck, or if I'm here talking to a duck because I haven't eaten. I need to be eating. But everything tastes like barf or dust or makes my stomach burn.

"I'm sorry to tell you this. I know it's not great information. But you deserve honesty. This is all I know."

The cops didn't seem to think there was much to do. They told me they searched the park. They told me the case was open. They told me nothing after the second day. Then they went back to patrolling the big park and the small parks too, looking for people who can't afford to live anywhere else making a space for themselves, or people trying to find pleasure in the darkness. The park must be pristine for the tourists and runners and rich people living in new high-rises. The people who keep this city at its knees and alive. The cops don't give a shit about him.

"Duck, are you really talking to me?"

"Rude."

"Sorry. Thank you. You're the only one who's really helped."

The duck briefly presses its beak to my leg, then flies away.

My phone bleeps. I haven't had a lot of messages in the past few days. Everyone is already tired of checking on me. I look down at the screen. My mom. Texting me to call. Instead of calling. She's learned how to communicate in the modern age. She can wait. She's not tired of checking on me yet. She might be obsessed with it. I start back toward the building-lined streets of the West End.

I scroll down and look through our communications. Over and over again, our same phrase to check on each other:

Are you alive?

A text to be sent on its own. No added emojis, no grocery store requests, no emotional outpourings of any kind. Just a single question.

Everything else is all over the place. Scrolling through our texts is like looking at an unfinished art project. The blue and white lines vary in length depending on the level of anxiety, the retreat of the depression, the blunt blips of physical pain. My responses sometimes go on too long. I've always worried that if I don't text back enough reassurance, information, love, something bad will happen in that moment. So clearly my messaging skills are poor. Where the fuck is he?

"Where the fuck are you?" I whisper to my reflection in the blacked-out windows of a shuttered clothing store.

There's no answer. Just me shuffling from foot to foot in these flip-flops I bought a week before the note. He was with me on that shopping trip. Sort of. In that way he'd started to be: physically present, occasionally interjecting with monosyllabic responses or his finger briefly pressed into the small of my back as we walked, but his mind anywhere but near. I'd rented a car share to take us to the new weird-ass mall in the sunken suburb.

He'd wanted to be alone that day, to watch the daily horrors and sublimely simple human-interest stories of the Sunday morning news. But I shut off the TV and stood holding the remote until he looked at me.

"Nettie."

"That is one of my nicknames, yes."

A grumble. "I wanted to watch that."

"I got a car. We're going shopping. You can listen to the radio, we can pretend it's the olden days. I'll let you run the dial."

"It's digital."

"True. See, you're already talking about the potentials of the trip."

He rolled over on the couch and winced. I went to the bedroom and grabbed his favourite T-shirt, soft from years of wear, and his loosest jeans. When his body hurt, he only wanted to wear flannel pyjamas and loose sweatshirts, but we were going outside.

I shut the blinds and placed the clothes on the couch near his head. Then I clapped my hands a few times, like I was trying to get the attention of a room of preschoolers. He stayed a solid, unmoving lump. I jammed my knuckles near his shoulder blades, a pressure point for him, a sore spot among many sore spots. I did this for ten minutes, rolling knuckles and elbows over his back. My own shoulders sting from years of these motions. I only ever treat myself to a massage once a year. Coverage at work isn't the best for either of our medical needs.

After I finished, he sat up and gave me a brief hug, then started to get dressed. Once he got his shirt on, he stopped and looked at me like I'd injured him.

"I'm not wearing underwear."

"On purpose?" I said, winking.

But I went back to the bedroom and got him a pair from the drawer. Tropical fish print. The kind I picked out for him, not the grey kind in three-packs he got himself.

Before the note, he had gotten dressed, I assume, and left while I was at work, so I couldn't describe what he was wearing. I seemed negligent. A shitty wife. I had to look at which clothes were left behind to piece together what he might be wearing. A grey shirt, like always.

When I get home from the wood duck conversation, I open Word and create a missing poster.

Missing

Tall sad man with short sandy hair.

No one saw him leave, but he is probably wearing clothes. Like, jeans and a grey sweatshirt.

I find a photo of him and make sure he's not smiling in it. I don't want anyone who sees him to get the wrong idea. I will put these up in the morning. Just in case he's run off, not dead. He is pretty slow. Even a week later, he can't have gotten far. I'll write a new to-do list. Like today, like every day until I can think again.

I wake up from a nap to my phone ringing. After the day I've had, I wonder if it's the duck calling me. He had a lot to say.

"Honey, you can come home. Your old bedroom is ready—we never turned it into a den or a craft room or a gym. I keep the elliptical and the stationary tandem bike and the BowFlex and the ThighMaster and all the rest in that dark corner of the basement. Annetta, everything's here for you."

It's funny to think any of these things might be in their home. She's just listing items other mothers have used to replace their children in their empty nests.

It's not like he was raking in money, but living alone in the most expensive city in Canada isn't going to be easy. Especially when I have no idea how long I won't be working. I don't know how long my bereavement pay lasts. I do know that five years ago, when my grandmother died, I got three days, and it wasn't enough to go back for the funeral, so I had to use some vacation time, and I got stuck in a storm, because of course grey skies and funerals are a delightful combination.

"Mom, I'm good. I don't need to come home because I'm in my home right now. I've lived here for like twenty-five years."

"Well, you've only been renting that place for eight years. Your place before for three and a half and the other place for one year and then you lived with those girls for five. That seemed so fun."

"You're right, my entire adult life should add up to an even number, not an odd one. Funny that."

"Annetta."

"Mom."

"I think you are a fine person, and I only want to help you."

"I want to talk about other things. And live here for now. I'll visit you soon. Tell me what you're doing."

"Well, I miss the old host, but there is a lot going on in this episode."

While she recounts the latest episode of *60 Minutes*, I pull up my email and look at my bill payments, student loans. Our shared bank account looks normal, but mine is a mess. The face creams I bought are stashed away in the Christmas decorations box in the storage room in the basement. The expensive dinners were long ago digested and flushed down the toilet. Documented on ImageScroller, which he never used, so he never saw the golden beet purée drizzled on mint quinoa. The bottles of wine, craft beer, fifty-five dollar cocktails, all consumed. He couldn't track what I was doing in plain sight because he wasn't paying attention.

"Do you think the wildfires are going to start earlier this year? Are we in a good place with weather?"

"The fires are coming like always, but hopefully rain too. A lot of rain."

"Six months of fire?"

"It's possible. Every year it lasts longer. Becomes more possible."

I can't stop myself from walking to the park every morning. You hear a talking duck one time and then you have to go back to where the talking duck was every time you go walking. I examine every wood duck and feel awful that they all look the same to me. I'm an asshole who can't tell the difference between these beautiful individual creatures.

Along the back side of the lagoon, the apartments of the West End are visible, the taller buildings of Coal Harbour. I keep my eyes on the water's edge, watching the surface for any lone wood ducks. A woman in head-to-toe yoga gear speed-walks past me with her dog bounding on a leash beside her. I trip, the toe of my shoe caught on a rock, and I try and fail to stop myself from splashing into the lagoon, which is very unfit for humans, being so full of bird shit and E. coli. It's not deep, but it's cold and gross and I slip around on slimy rocks trying to crawl up the short bank. Luckily, only my lower half is wet. I grip the bullrushes and pull myself up, then grab at the dry rocks near the trail until I'm upright again.

I take a moment to look around. I'm close to the footbridge where ducks often hang out, waiting for tourists to toss them fancy snacks. There's a bench, and I sit, take a moment. A memorial plaque on the bench is "Dedicated to our beloved Jackson 'Jacko' and his beloved pooch Sal. May they both watch the birds from their favourite perch."

I take a photo of the memorial. Maybe I want one for him: "Hey! Please come home, husband, if you're not dead! Thanks!" I open ImageScroller to post the plaque in my stories, adding a GIF of a dog with text that reads "Good Boy!" And then for the first time since he's been gone, I open my camera app with the front camera on and facing me. My face looks less distressed than I thought it would. I hold the phone above my head and take a selfie. My first pseudo-widow selfie.

"Of course. A selfie."

I look around but don't see anyone. The woman and her dog have moved onto another trail. I smell something, though, like a musk. An old-fashioned cologne. Something rattles the leaves of a nearby salmonberry bush. A long, fluffy tail pops out, like a showgirl jumping out of a cake.

"I'm not judging you. I like selfies."

A grey-and-brown squirrel scampers over to the bench and climbs up onto an armrest. Its head moves back and forth a few times and its tail fluffs and flutters, like it has a shiver.

"I wanted to remember what I look like." This time, I don't question it. Better talk to this squirrel now in case it changes its mind about talking to me at all. The squirrel jumps to the top of the bench and places a small paw on my arm. "Living alone is weird. I could just be looking for attention." *Aren't we all?* I think.

"Aren't we all?" the squirrel says.

I should get up off this bench, go home, clean myself off before whatever it is in the bird-shit-laced lagoon gets into my bloodstream, clogs up my pores, invades me, and does whatever it'll do to my health. But there's a squirrel talking to me, and I don't want to mess this up. I can't remember what the wood duck even looked like, and we might never talk again, so I have to take my opportunities when they show up.

"Are you ..."

"Clairvoyant? Yes, I am. Thank you for noticing. A lot of animals are. Some choose to ignore it, though. A lack of interest or just a callousness about others, really."

"Oh, interesting."

The squirrel dashes onto the leg of my soaking-wet jeans and looks up at me, as though they're going to clasp my face in their tiny paws and force me to hear something deep.

"Listen, lady. I get it. You're struggling. But so are we all. I know you're still looking. But are you really?" I cross my arms, stare out at a willow tree. A heron lands underneath it and disappears into the foliage. "And if you are looking, what are you looking for?"

I turn away, my eyes trained on the path to Second Beach, an escape.

The squirrel jumps onto my crossed arms. I jerk back around just as they wind up and slap their little clawed paw across my cheek.

"Snap out of it! Pay attention! I'm not usually this aggressive. Look at me, okay?" I lower my head to make better eye contact with the squirrel. "I know you think I'm some figment of your imagination and that you're out here looking for him, but really, that's not it at all. Okay? But I know you will find what you're looking for. Believe me."

A man and a dachshund come trotting around the corner. The dog looks up at the squirrel and starts to get that dog look, getting ready to chase. But the squirrel gives the dog the finger and then the dog lags behind the man, trotting more slowly, so the man has to tug the leash. The squirrel gets back on my lap, tail puffed up, and we both sit quietly until they pass.

"I should be going." The squirrel hops off me, back to the salmonberry bush.

"Sorry. This is probably weird. Can I take a photo of you?"

"Yes, no video, though. I don't talk on camera. I have to maintain some mystique."

The squirrel is serene now, though still a bit intimidating. But in a way that demands respect. It cups its hands around the stalks of the bush, its fuzzy face nestled in the fresh flowering buds. I snap a photo straight into my ImageScroller story.

"Thank you," I say, as the squirrel scampers off farther into the park.

A week after our last chat, I get an email from Li. Not even a text, definitely not a phone call. She's putting me on leave for another three weeks at least. The company is insisting. She's sorry, but also she will see me soon, because we're supposed to go shopping tomorrow. Whatever. I turn my phone off. No one I need to talk to. Unless they're a furry or feathered animal—then I'll consider it.

No one else has sent me a message in four days. If people don't want to check on me, they don't have to. But I feel like they should want to hang out with me. At least Li does, wants to. I tried to cancel this shopping trip, not sure I was in the mood, but Li said that was a bad attitude to take. And I listen to her.

Shopping with her is the best, because she doesn't judge, not even my worst spending. Capitalistic therapy. Though, of course, she doesn't know about every purchase I make. Like when I freaked out and bought three pairs of the exact same style of loose linen jumpsuit, so instead of looking like I was spending too much on mid-priced jumpsuits, I looked like a gross person who wore the same seemingly unwashed jumpsuit all the time.

Today, we each decide to get the most outrageous casual wear we can find, because it will supposedly help us to relax, even though it never really works. Li picks a soft striped romper. I go all in on a floral sweatsuit. Then we head to the food court and sit as far away from other people as possible. Nibbling from each other's plates of noodles.

"Okay, so this guy said he was a freelancer, but he would never tell me what kind. So even though I loved his dick, I had to stop seeing him. I felt like I was compromising. I act like I just want to bone down, but I do like talking to people."

"I know, that's why you're great!"

"And then that other guy kept saying he would come over, but then he'd stop at the entrance to my building, and I could see him outside, but he would never come up."

"That's horrible. I don't like that he knows where you live."

"I don't either."

We sip our fountain pop, impressed that straws have made a comeback. These ones are made of corn and taste a little like it. A good match for the corn syrup in the drinks.

"The food court is weirdly relaxing."

"Agreed. Though this one is getting a bit too fancy. Too many fast-food grain bowls."

"Li, you're so right."

We decide to do one more sweep to look at uncomfortable shoes that we might once have foolishly put on our feet. Both of us go for Hush Puppies now, maybe Geox.

"I can't believe you almost didn't get that sweatsuit. I can't believe you almost didn't come out today."

"With you, I always say yes, though."

"That's why I love you."

I've always been jealous of Li's divorce. It's made her a better, much cooler person. And she let go on her own terms. She made a choice and stuck with it.

"Want a ride home?" she asks.

In the back of my mind, all I can think about is ducks and squirrels. Maybe I should make a trip to the park, just in case.

"No, I'd rather walk."

I leave Li at the entrance to the parkade. Walk the twenty blocks to the lagoon. Do three laps. The ducks swim in their little groups, the squirrels steer clear of me. There is goose shit along the entire path and there are geese every twenty feet. No one talks to me. No one looks at me. I keep thinking I'll feel his presence, but I feel nothing of the kind.

I wake up and curl into the duvet, stare at my phone. It's been three weeks and I haven't talked to my parents once. My bedroom smells like stale sweat, and there are a million texts from Li.

Why aren't you messaging me back?
Are you coming back to work?

I'm supposed to, but I don't want to. Over the last three weeks, I've been to the lagoon three times a day, tracing its edge three times each, and nothing has come of it. Nothing has happened. I'm still here doing the same thing, without different results. I've made no plans. Done nothing. My daily to-do list has been stuck on "talk to Li about going back to work" and "go to the bank." I don't plan to do either. I turn off my phone.

I can see a shirt peeking out from the closet. Part of a sleeve. I've been wearing only the same four pieces of clothing. Once I washed the lagoon jeans, I decided to wear them every time I entered the park. But they're not working. Maybe I washed something special off of them. Maybe there was magic vomit on there, a bit of his sweat, or something else entirely.

I get up and go to the closet. It's brimming with my clothes, but the shirt sleeve sticking out is his. His one shirt for the rare occasions when we had to go to a nice thing—a wedding, a party. I fold the sleeve in and try to close the door, but it won't shut all the way. I push harder, knocking myself to the ground. It still doesn't close. I whip it open again and start pulling out my things. The dresses, the jumpsuits, the blouses and scarves, tote bag after tote bag, each one containing more tote bags inside. A mountain of clothes beside me. Realizing I haven't changed the sheets since he left, I strip the bed before using it to organize each piece from the pile. So many things I bought out of sadness, and now they all have a sadness to them. Each one is a flash of memories from when I needed to feel more than despair, but none of it worked. I put back the items I'm keeping, the closet now a clearer picture. His shirts are neat, not jumbled up and nearly displaced by mine. I slip the clothes I'll donate into tote bags from within the other tote bags. I make the bed with fresh sheets and bring the rank ones down to the shared laundry room. Before I put them in the washer, I inhale them, rub a corner of his pillowcase against my cheek. There's nothing left of him there. His essence is already gone.

Back upstairs, I shower and moisturize my face for the first time in a month. I place the face creams in the medicine cabinet and pull out all the prescriptions. I put on my new sweatsuit, climb into the freshly made bed, and organize the bottles, his and mine, making a little house out of his on his bedside table. I crawl out to put the sheets in the dryer, and when I return to bed I eye the Klonopin I was given after he went missing. I haven't taken one this whole time. I take three.

I wake up under a tree.

My hair is covered in leaves, my face smeared with something sticky—I don't know what it is, and if I find out, I'll probably be disgusted. I can hear splashing somewhere near me. A beach ball lands on my chest. It reads "TD BANK! LOVE IS LOVE!" Promotional Pride swag from a bank. Is this a sign that I finally need to deal with my banking? I tap the pockets of my sweatsuit and realize I don't have my phone with me, just my keys and a half-eaten granola bar crumpled and melted in my left fist.

"Over here!"

Another splash. I sit up, check myself. No blood, and I'm not soaking wet this time, thank fuck.

"Hi Annetta. Sorry. I couldn't tell if you were sleeping or just maybe had too many Mike's Hard Lemonades."

A raven-haired mermaid is swishing her tail in the murky lagoon water, her long hair floating behind her.

"I don't drink Mike's Hard Lemonade. I'm not fourteen. Or at the PNE."

She flips over onto her side and stretches one arm out of the water. "Well, I don't know. There are always empty bottles with that label left all over this place. A duck got trapped in one last week."

"I know a duck! A talking duck!" I shout.

"There are a lot of talking ducks, woman. Anyway, sorry to offend. People love to drink in public and leave their trash."

"That makes sense. I'm not mad at you. Sorry if I was defensive about that type of alcohol. It's classist. Ageist. It's a bad attitude. I've been accused of having a bad attitude. A lot more lately, but also in general."

She flips her hair up and out of the water, and tiny droplets fling off in all directions, refracting rainbows. I check the position of the sun, as if I really know how to tell time without my phone.

"Okay, so you're a mermaid. This is new. I mean, okay. Okay."

She swims closer to me, her eyes black and shiny, her skin sleek and brown.

"Everyone always thinks that sculpture on the other side of the park is like me. But it's called *Girl in Wetsuit,* for crying out loud."

"I'm sorry, I'm sure I've made that mistake."

"Well, we all make mistakes. Even me. Once I tried to save a guy who fell out of a sailboat and was thrashing around in False Creek. I was about to swim him to safety when I heard a woman on the boat telling someone she'd just pushed her would-be rapist out of the boat, so luckily I let him go and left him there. But that was a close one."

"Oh wow. That is quite a story. I'm fascinated. I have so many questions overall. I'm sorry. I may have taken a lot of Klonopin."

"That's okay. I'm not judging you."

I remember reading a book about aquatic cryptids years ago. Mermaids are associated with perilous events. Seems obvious to point out that I find losing my husband and mysteriously passing out beside a lagoon to be perilous events. And yet, I don't feel like I'm in peril now.

The mermaid twirls around, her tail peeking out of the water, spraying droplets as she swims and dips. I feel like I'm staring. It's hard not to stare at a mermaid. She's so huge and so light, at least ten feet in length, buoyant and beautiful.

"Can I ask a question? I feel like I'm never prepared to ask questions when ducks or squirrels are talking to me."

"Yes, thank you for asking. And sometimes it's not easy to talk to a duck. Squirrels are terrible listeners. Neither are that into conversation, and sometimes I feel they just like to hear themselves talk."

"Why haven't I been able to talk to those animals again, and why are they so quick to leave me, and why doesn't anyone have any answers? I want to know who gets around the most. Which of these animals is patrolling the most, and who's the biggest busybody and gets all the gossip around here? How am I supposed to get anything done when I feel like I'm missing everything? Am I bad at everything? Is my husband really dead, and does that even matter?"

The mermaid dives below the surface of the water. Is she gone? Has she left me? Did I overwhelm her? I didn't get any answers. I see nothing, not even a ripple. I move over to the edge of the lagoon, crouch on a grouping of small stones. Then she jumps clear out of the water, like Ariel, easing her perfect Disney body out of the sea and onto the land's edge, beside me.

"These are all good questions. Though actually I don't love answering questions. I'm supposed to be cryptic. I just happen to have a lot of knowledge. You should try and let go of some of these questions. Say something definitive instead. I like to whisper things to myself to test them out. They sound so much quieter underwater."

She drapes an arm over my shoulder and leans her sopping wet head to mine. I wince at first, but she smells so fresh and minty, like she's made of gum. I reach my arm around her other side and squeeze her shoulder. We sit and watch a family of ducks swimming past, fresh yellow baby fluffs. I sigh. She laughs loudly. A tinkling of pure joy at something so sweet as a duckling. I curl into her body and start to cry on her wet shoulder. I sob until my face is soaked from my own tears and not her moist skin. She lets me lean my full weight against her. I cry until my face feels hot and dry. Then I sit up. She places a cupped hand delicately on either side of my face, leans in close.

"You should be going, right?" I say to her.

"Yes. You're really getting it."

"One more question?"

"Sure."

"How can you swim in there? Isn't it full of things that make people sick?"

"I'm magic, bitch. I can swim wherever I want."

She flips daintily back into the lagoon. I watch her rapidly leap in and out of the water until she looks like a small trout jumping for a fly. Then she disappears.

I don't know what's going to happen. He is gone and I am here, and I'm figuring things out, but it's slow. It takes time. I hope the animals will still talk to me. I hope Li will too.

I stand up and walk deeper into the forest to find a quiet spot. I kneel down, push my face into the bushes, press my cheek to the ground and whisper, "I want him to know that I hate this. I know he's gone. I just hate it. And I hate that I can't tell him. And I'm sorry for all the times I made him wear hard pants."

My chest feels light again. It still hurts, but less. Like I'm carrying a small ball bearing instead of a lead balloon. I roll onto my back on the earth and stare up into the canopy. I feel my hands unclench.

Her bus trip is as uneventful as the train ride. One person gets on for a single stop. She takes it one farther and gets off the number 84 six blocks from their old apartment. There's still an apartment building there, but it's not really where they used to live. The insides are gutted, the spaces made smaller. Her bedroom is now a solarium / den / office space. Why she looks at realty listings online, she doesn't really know. It's embarrassing for a fourteen-year-old. But she wants to know what happened to her old life. Seems pretty typical: more suites with less space. The stickers she left on the bathroom mirror are definitely gone, tossed into a dumpster along with the old wall-mounted sink and leaky toilet. The new mirror has special lighting and a finish that makes it easier to wipe clean. She knows every unit has a bidet now. She heads downhill. The walk is chilly closer to the water, morning breeze blowing in a storm. As she turns onto her old street, the wind knocks down her hood, but she pulls it back on. Car headlights flash, and she cuts into an alley. Their unit was on the alley side.

DIRTY DEEDS DONE DIRT CHEAP

"Can you clean up in there? There's urine all over the place. Like, a lot of urine. It's disgusting." Allie is rushing to get to her first meeting when a tall person in a charcoal suit stops her, pointing at the washroom door and shouting desperately about urine. Allie isn't late, but she's committed to being early. She started at Platinum Corp last week, and assistant jobs in the downtown core are hard to come by, even for someone who's been a professional assistant for ten years. The executive assistant game is competitive. Not lucrative, but certainly better than a lot of options for someone with a liberal arts degree without experience making latte art.

"I'm a junior executive assistant," she sputters at the person. Though she doesn't think anyone should talk to someone who has to clean urine for a living using that tone. Custodians already know urine is disgusting. But maybe this is what's expected of her. Or maybe her beige-toned jumpsuit is too reminiscent of a sanitation worker's uniform. Bland colours are so popular in professional settings. She holds her tablet tightly to her chest and moves through the open office. Her desk is in an attached row with the other assistants' desks, alongside a bank of filing cabinets that obscures their view of the windows overlooking the mountains. Behind them are the offices of the managers and the junior and senior executives.

Every job has eccentricities, new expectations, a broadened scope of what it means to assist. The last job was good until it felt like she was being buried in papers—funny in an increasingly paperless work landscape. Until her boss started to sexually harass her in a way no boss of hers ever had before. He'd even torn her blouse, like a stereotype of a bad boss in a 1980s movie. His nickname for her when no one was around made her hate certain baked goods. Knowing it would get her nowhere to do anything about it, she entered his office as infrequently as possible, always leaving the door open, and took all her vacation time and her few sick days.

A friend who works in accounting tipped her off about this position, and she rushed to update her CV and scrub clean her already pretty tidy social media. The position paid more and was closer to her co-op building in Railtown. The interview lasted three days. She had to balance a tray of pastries while discreetly carrying confidential paperwork, take a call on the move while calculating the tip on a lunch meeting order, move from one floor to the one above via the stairs in under two minutes. They had her trim a spider plant, compose fifty emails in an hour, then print and shred them. This office has the most high-tech shredder. It mulches the paper. She passed the test, quit her old job with no notice, and started this one the next day. She'd never done that before. It felt scary and exhilarating.

The boardroom is cozier than expected. Small, well lit, facing the corner with ocean and mountains. The perfect combination. A little distracting, a little inspiring. Her boss, Lucien, whom she's met only once, is seated near the door, and she nods politely as she walks in. He doesn't notice her. Everyone on their floor is scheduled to be in today's meeting, even junior executive assistants. Her boss's boss, Mr. Alan Peterson, stands in front of the mountain landscape at the head of the long boardroom. His suit is loudly patterned, like maybe he looks up to Don Cherry. Allie stands near the wall, blending into the paint.

"Welcome, everyone. Please settle. We have a lot to cover today and not a lot of time. I'm flying out at 11 a.m. I need everyone ready to launch our new project. The word is going out tomorrow, and we've had more than enough time to prepare. I want everyone to know the talking points, to understand where we're coming from, and to be able to do their jobs in service to this project."

Allie takes notes on her workplace-issued tablet. The project is innovative. The project is brand enhancing. The project is impressive in its simplicity. Allie doesn't know what any projects are yet. All she's done so far is to sit quietly and answer emails and keep those who've scheduled meetings with Paul from actually getting to have those meetings. The Residential Tenancy Branch has been turned away three times. They reiterate that they have an appointment, Allie apologizes and reschedules, and the cycle continues. They keep leaving cards, which she stashes in a drawer in a tin that says "You Got This!" with a cartoon squirrel giving a thumbs-up. She's spent the rest of her time dropping paperwork into the paper-shredding receptacle, and when it's full, which is often, she emails the industrial shredding company. They show up within two hours to take it away.

At the end of the meeting, she dashes after Lucien, who shakes hands with all the senior executives and managers as they leave, and stays silent beside him, just off to the side.

"Hello, sir."

"Arley," Lucien says.

"Allie."

"Ah yes. Sorry, we've had quite a turnaround on assistants lately. So many just not up to the task, buried in work. But your resumé was impeccable, and your interview was impressive. I hope you'll be able to stick around. I feel confident we made a great choice."

He starts to walk toward his office, and she follows.

"I'm glad you came to find me. We'll need to introduce you to the person you'll be working with on the new project," he says.

"Of course. I'm excited to be here."

She is ready for new tasks. She likes that so far her boss has barely taken an interest in her. They pass by her desk row and enter his office.

"Lotus!" he shouts, stepping through the door.

A taut woman with a pale pinched face, thin nude lips, and a tight blond bun steps out from behind a swivel chair. Her jumpsuit is black and tight and compliments her long, thin gold necklaces, which match the gold heels on her black ankle boots.

"Oh, beautiful. Just beautiful. You're here. You're both here. Is this the one? The one we're going to work with? Just fabulous. Hello, I'm Lotus." She reaches out a hand for Allie to shake, then quickly retracts it and loops a finger through her delicate moon-shaped pendant. She looks like a corporate witch.

"Hello, I'm Allie. Great to meet you. Uh, what ..."

"Lotus is the project manager on a very specific part of this project," Lucien says. He nods his head and smiles widely at both women like he's proud to have the two of them working together. "Now, if you two could take this somewhere else, I've got a synergy project consult to do in here. And, Allie, excellent work so far thwarting all those useless meetings with safety commissioners and housing organizations. Booking the meetings is an olive branch. There's no time to actually have them. But someone does reach out to them, rest assured. We are in direct contact. We are very concerned with community engagement."

Lotus turns and stamps her way out of the office at an incredible clip. Again, Allie follows along, trailing behind until they get to Lotus's office, a small nook near the washroom. Inside, it's stark black and white with gold accents. Her desk shiny and white, the chair white leather, the bookshelves black and filled with books with their spines turned away and their page edges sprayed gold, and on the corner of her desk and in the windowsill are fake plants also painted gold. Her outfit and pale skin fit right into her workspace.

She sits in her white-leather chair and motions for Allie to take a seat on a sculptural human form in repose, presumably also a chair.

"Do you have any gardening experience? I believe on your resumé it said you did?"

"Oh yes, I do. I did some landscaping work when I was a student."

"Just beautiful. So yeah, gardening will be part of your job now. I hope that's okay. We pay a higher wage for this grade of assistant for a reason. There is some physical labour. You'll be in the office Monday, Tuesday, Wednesday, and in the garden Thursday and Friday."

Allie nods vigorously. She didn't expect to be doing physical labour, but there were physical and endurance tests in the interview.

"Gardening is very relaxing. Hard work but enjoyable, nice, contemplative. I'll be happy to do it."

Lotus has seemingly already moved on to something else, phone in hand, face tight with concern. "Oh shit. I mean great. Oh sorry. I should control my profanity until we know each other better. Just got some annoying news. You know how it is. So, continue what you're doing for the next few days, and I'll email you the details of where to meet me on Thursday for our big first day in the field."

And then she's turned her back to Allie to make a call, her bun like a cloud against the blue sky visible through the window. By the time Allie gets back to her desk, Outlook already has a meeting notification for Thursday.

She spends the rest of her day trying to clear her to-do list, knowing she has less time to finish her office tasks now that she'll be working off-site two days a week. She responds to as many emails as possible and cancels meetings on her calendar for the next few Thursdays and Fridays, then moves on to the spreadsheet list of donors still to be contacted about the former CEO's memorial crosswalk, set to go on the street outside the building's front doors. By the time she looks up and away from her computer, it's dark outside, and all she's eaten is the dust of the cashews she keeps hidden in her top desk drawer.

She shuts down her workstation and packs up her shoulder bag with her uneaten lunch and the sweater she needs to combat the frigid air conditioning. It won't be the first time she's eaten her lunch on her walk home. Then she hears a loud voice from down the hall and running footsteps coming toward the open office.

A young woman in a "LET'S ROYALLY FUCK UP THE MAYOR" T-shirt bursts in. "Let me talk to Mr. Peterson!" she shouts. When she turns around, the back of the shirt shows the mayor's bloody head flying out of a guillotine.

Trailing her are two security guards, but she's spry and jumps over an entire row of desks, stopping right near Allie.

"Mr. Peterson—where is he?" she asks Allie.

"He's gone. He had to fly out early this morning."

"Well, shit."

"Can I give him a message?" Allie asks, holding up a tablet and digipen.

"Yeah, tell him he sucks shit!"

The security guards come around either side of where they are in the bank of desks, and the taller one grabs the young woman by her wrists, the other by her ankles. They say nothing to Allie as they carry her out of the office, toward the freight elevators, not the ones in the front.

"You fucking jerkasses! Two more housing activists are missing! Tell your fucking boss that!" the young woman screams as she's carted away.

Allie tosses down her tablet and pen, grabs her jacket and bag, and leaves quickly.

As soon as Allie gets off the bus at the corner of Macdonald and West 4th Avenue, she sees the huge sign staked into the ground.

> **The newest Platinum Corp experience will grow here!**
>
> Platinum Corp is installing premium garden beds for a temporary natural enhancement until we're ready to start building! So, while we wait to create incredible housing, take this opportunity to grow you own food, flowers, and so much more!
>
> Brought to you by Platinum Corp Community™ Garden #2

Below the text on the billboard is an illustration of green vines growing into a forty-storey condo that rises into the clouds. The Platinum Corp community garden is spread thinly over an expensive tract of land that used to be a gas station. Nowadays, most gas stations are outside the city limits, leaving only a few stray ones either unable to sell or too profitable to unload, since anyone in the city centre who still owns a car is desperate not to drive twenty kilometres to get gas. The rich people have all bought electric Voltas, and charging stations are where the real money is. These former gas station lots are perfect for luxury condos, but by law they can't build on a site where oil and gas might have leached into the ground for at least a few years. Somehow, community gardens are permitted, though. Growing things you might eat is fine, but no concrete foundations.

Allie can't find an entrance in the chain-link fence around the perimeter. She goes back where she came from and finally notices an open gate along the alley side. Inside the garden are large identical raised plots, half a metre wide by two metres long. Numbered and perfectly spaced from each other, they look to be newly built. The wooden edging around each plot smells good. She walks over and looks inside one. Empty. They're all empty.

Lotus is standing near a small wooden shed, holding a clipboard and a pair of gardening gloves. "Al! Over here!" She hands Allie the gloves and unlocks the shed. Inside is a wide variety of shiny tools. "Have you come by here before?"

"Not to the garden, no. But this spot, sure. I grew up thinking I'd never own a car. And I don't. But I remember this gas station. It was near where a friend from university lived, and we would get pop, chips, and cigarettes from there."

"Smoking! Are you a bad girl, Allie? Just kidding, I used to smoke too. God, wish I still did. Maybe I'll start again!" She reaches into her pocket and pulls out a ring with two keys. "These are yours now. They open the gate and this shed."

Walking around to the side of the shed, she points to a tower of bagged soil, some sacks of fertilizer, and five wheelbarrows loaded with plants.

"Everything you need should be here. Now, just make this whole place your own. We'll drop things off here, so when you get in on Thursday and Friday mornings, everything will be ready for you. And that's it. Ideally, they'd like this done within two weeks. Then when the next project rolls around, we'll move on to that."

That's it. Just plant an entire billion-dollar lot full of perennials and squash in two weeks. No big deal.

"So, this is a community garden?"

"Yup, for the community to enjoy. But they can't have a plot. If they try to enroll, they'll get a notification that it's at capacity."

"But … um …"

Lotus's phone pings. She puts up her hand to stop Allie from talking while she angrily sends a voice note: "Listen, I don't have more time to spend on this right now. If you feel like you can't take this on, we can easily find someone else." Her phone keeps pinging away, she rapidly responds and sighs.

"I've got this," Allie says. "No need to worry."

"Beautiful! If you finish early, just head home. They'll drop off more supplies before you start tomorrow. No need to come into the office on these days. Obviously you'll be covered in this shit, so."

Lotus doesn't finish her thought, just takes off in her gold muumuu and backless black mules.

Allie slips on her gloves, empties a wheelbarrow of plants, and replaces them with as many bags of soil as she can carry. After her first attempt, she knows how much soil she'll need for each plot: five bags. There are equal amounts of orange and red marigolds, green and yellow zucchini, a selection of herbs, and thankfully some wildflower seeds to spread around. To make it appear like individuals have planted here, she'll have to be strategic and place things a little imperfectly.

She's hasn't used fertilizer much before—it's fallen out of favour, and everyone is going with compost instead—but she decides to use what she's been given. They must want her to. She grabs a bag. The packages are marked with the same image of vines growing into a condo building towering in the sky. Of course they've branded their own fertilizer. She spreads some over the green stems and under the leaves of the squash. The texture is off; the tiny pellets are soft, not rough like she'd expect. The back of the package says it's made from a mix of mulched paper. "We want to make office waste grow into something new!" The paper is completely pulped and pressed and covered in dirt. She hopes these are just shredded emails and not part of some conspiracy to fudge numbers.

As she's about to head home, she gets a message from Lotus:

Pics or it didn't happen LOL

Allie snaps a shot of one of the planters and sends it. She gets no response.

By the end of Friday, she's not through even a quarter of the plots. Lotus admits it's a bigger job than she, someone with a black thumb, had anticipated. All of Allie's office work is on hold until she finishes, and she has one week to get the whole job done.

"The end of next week?" Allie says, her hands deep in manure.

"Or else, ha ha ha ha!" Lotus chortles over the phone.

On Monday, Allie starts gardening full-time. At least her benefits will cover 80 percent of the cost of five massages. She'll need them. Who will keep Lucien's meetings from happening? Every time a housing advocate wanders onto their floor, Allie is supposed to give them free coffee and a coupon for protein bars at the café downstairs. She didn't do that the last time, on Wednesday night.

For now, she has to get this garden done in a single week before she can go back to shooing away housing advocates and hiding business cards in a drawer. At the end of every day, she has to send Lotus photos of every finished plot. Thankfully, they've delivered new plants so that Allie can make the plots look "authentic and beautiful." Both words straight from Lotus's mouth.

It's warmer than anticipated for a March morning, and by 11 a.m., Allie's drenched in sweat. She wishes this were still a convenience store. She's brought a bottle of water, but a sports drink would be perfect. Reminding her of youth and of hangovers. She locks up and heads down the street to a small corner shop.

"I'm sorry I'm so dirty. Could you just grab me a blue Gatorade and I'll tap my card? I don't want to get everything in your store covered in filth."

"You part of that community garden?" the cashier asks.

"Yeah. I mean, I'm working on it, yeah."

"We tried to apply for a plot, but there was no information online. It just said 'coming soon.' And nothing else. Very strange to me."

Allie taps her card and nods in agreement.

"Yes, it is strange. Thank you."

"Oh, hello."

A young man in a Platinum Corp crewneck sweatshirt startles Allie. It's dark out, she wasn't expecting anyone to come, and she keeps the gate locked while she works. Thankfully, there was a headlamp in the shed, and the garden is lit by the lights on the billboard. She's working late, having decided to move some plants for better visuals and "authenticity." She just wants to get finished so she can go back to wearing business casual and not have to worry about developing a stoop.

"I didn't know anyone would still be here," the man says. "They said the girl leaves by five-thirty at the latest."

Allie assumes she is "the girl." She finishes digging a hole for potatoes and stands up. "Hi, I'm Allie. An adult woman." She smiles at him.

The young guy doesn't smile or introduce himself. He flips a set of keys in his hand. Like her keys, they're attached to a gold-vined Platinum Corp key chain.

"Well, I'll wait in the van until you're done and then make my drop-offs."

"You don't have to do that, I'm almost finished. You can do whatever you need to do now."

But he's already on his way back to the alley, where a plain white van is parked.

Allie nestles a potato plant into place and then hustles out of the garden, locking the gate behind her. As she rounds the corner, she sees the van turn around and back up closer to the gate.

At the bus stop, she checks her phone. She's missed peak time and will have to wait twenty minutes. She reaches for her bag and realizes she left it in the garden. If she rushes back, she can get it before the bus shows up. Otherwise it'll be forty minutes before she gets on her bus.

She runs back across the street and through the alley, grabbing for her keys, but the door is open. The young man is still there, loading a flatbed dolly with soil and fertilizer and some thicker black bags too.

"Sorry, forgot something. Oh, is that new stuff? Cool."

"What the fuck are you doing back here? Don't look at that."

"I'm just going to get my bag."

"Oh yeah, I found it. Be careful. Don't leave it behind next time." He holds out her bag. The zipper is open. "Saw you don't live in this area, so you'd better get going. It's getting late. Checked your ID to make sure it was yours. I coulda dropped it off later. Got the truck."

"Okay, thank you." Allie takes the bag from his outstretched hand, zips it closed, and runs back just in time to catch the bus home.

The next morning, everything looks like it always does: Fresh piles of soil, bags of fertilizer stacked in the exact same location, wheelbarrows full of plants. Her phone has an angry message from Lotus asking why she didn't send any new photos. Last night was so late and dark and that guy was so rude that Allie forgot. She sends an overly long apology email and fires off photos of three plots that she feels are looking the best.

She's actually enjoying this work, even though it's tiring. She catches herself squealing when she sees new flowers in the wheelbarrow. Maybe being paid a junior executive assistant's salary to play in dirt is a better deal than she thought.

Again, she'll have to redo some of the other plots. These new flowers will make them better, fuller, and more "authentic." There's a strange divot in one of the plots filled with wildflowers, one she finished two nights ago. Something is missing. Maybe someone broke in, climbed the fence to steal the snapdragons. It's a large hole, and to clean it up, she might as well redo the whole side of the garden.

As she digs, making a large mound, the soil smells loamier than usual, with an almost vinegar-like odour. Maybe that guy did something for the slugs. She's seen so many lately. Things are finally starting to look hopeful here—only five plots left to finish. For the last few, she wants to do herbs, lavender. If everything goes well and it doesn't rain too hard, and if her back holds out, she'll be done by Friday. Her most productive week of work ever.

She pushes the trowel deep into the ground and hears a crunch, like she's broken something. Is there a wooden barrier she's never noticed before? She stabs at the soil again, and there's another crunch. Pushing aside the soil with her fingers, she reaches down and makes contact with something thick, muscular. If it's a dead rat, she'll vomit. She uses the trowel to dig up the rest of the plants and then shovels out as much dirt as she can, until she starts to make out something light bluish, pinkish, in the ground.

She reaches down and grips it, yanks it out: a hand and half a forearm. She drops it immediately. Surprisingly, she doesn't vomit or cry, just stares at the disembodied piece of human anatomy. Eventually she walks into the shed and closes the door, then screams and kicks the wall, knocking the neatly displayed rakes and shovels to the ground. Her hands are shaking. After a few deep breaths she finds her phone in her bag and calls Lotus, who miraculously picks up.

"You've got one minute of my time, Al. What?"

"I'm sorry, I know you prefer messages, but it felt urgent. I just need to tell you that I found something strange in the garden. I got so excited about the snapdragons that I had to add some to one of the plots I thought was finished, and I was digging, and well, I just ..."

"What are you going on about?"

"I found an arm. A human arm."

"An arm? Please don't kid around less than a minute before my pre-meeting cleansing ritual. Retinol on the sphincter. They say not to, but it always perks me up."

"I was digging a hole to add some wildflowers and I hit something and when I reached in I pulled out an arm. It's not fake or a prosthetic. It's flesh. Human flesh, Lotus. I don't know what to do. Please tell me what I should do."

"Oh my god. Oh god. Grotesque. Not beautiful. That is not what we want. This is not what we want."

"I'm sorry, I'm sorry. I just thought this might be a crime scene. I figured it's best to let someone know, you know."

"Don't think about it again. But I mean, how could you not, right?"

"Okay, what should I do? I have so many more things to plant here."

There's a pause—Lotus has put her on hold. Or hung up. Allie walks back out to the garden, leaving her phone on speaker. She has to check again, confirm what she found. And there it is, tossed into the rich soil: part of a human arm.

"Hello, Allie? HELLO!"

"Yes, sorry, I'm here."

"Okay, listen to me. Don't do anything else. I'll come down and deal with this. I want you to go home. I'm going to order you some food. Vietnamese. Okay? Listen to me. I will deal with this. If we need you, I'll send a message. I've ordered you a VoltaShare."

"Oh. Okay. Thanks, Lotus."

"Beautiful."

Allie walks into her studio apartment and takes off her dirty work clothes, realizing she's worn her gloves the entire way in the VoltaShare. The gloves that touched dead human flesh. She tosses them in the bathroom garbage, on top of several days' worth of bloody tampons. This job could get her a bigger apartment in the co-op, maybe. A one-bedroom would be lovely. But the arm. All she can see is the arm. All she can think about is that the arm was attached to a person and now that person either has no arm, or that person is all the way dead. And no matter what, someone put that arm in there, definitely to hide it. It was put there after she had finished planting in that plot. Or after someone thought she'd finished.

That man with the van was so awful to her—the way he thrust her bag at her, the way he swore so sharply, even saying he would have dropped it off felt threatening. He sure didn't like that she'd shown up when she did, and he wanted her out of there, badly. Maybe so he could plant a body part in the soil, or multiple body parts. It was clear he'd been sent by Platinum Corp. Who else could have done it? And what should she do? The idea of quitting another job when every other job is terrible makes her want to vomit almost as much as working for someone who's using a community garden as a limb repository. Thinking about all of this makes her dizzy. Allie lies down on the rug beside her loveseat and curls into a ball.

Lotus messages that her food will be arriving in thirty minutes. Allie gets up off the floor and stares at her own naked flesh in the mirror for too long before getting into the shower, scrubbing her body, and washing her hair twice. She clips her fingernails as short as she can. Even though she was wearing the gloves, she can still feel her fingers pressing into the dead arm.

Hair in a towel, a robe tied around her, she waits in her lone kitchen chair, lacking the energy to dress herself. Delivery people have seen worse before. She's seen worse, today. Her buzzer rings, and she presses the entry button without asking who's there.

A minute later, a cheerful triple knock alerts her that someone's at the door. The person delivering food doesn't know she's had a bad day. So she puts on a smile, ready to be thankful. She opens the door.

The guy in the Platinum Corp crewneck is there, smiling now, a trowel in one hand. A length of rope in the other. Allie screams, but within seconds he's got the rope in her mouth and his knee on her neck. She can barely think, barely breathe. Another disorganized workplace cleaning up messes they made. She looks at her overflowing garbage bin, then closes her eyes.

The notice stands on two wooden posts. Seems so flimsy. "Application for Development." She drops her backpack to the ground and pulls out a can of paint, shakes it. A dog barks, and she turns to look, but in the early morning she can't see anything nearby. It's rare for anyone but dog walkers and runners to be out this early. Certainly, there are no cops in this area at this hour. It's a safe neighbourhood. Sanitized and clear. The paint is Clementine Fantasia. It reminds her of a soft drink her mom might have had in her day. The stencil took her a few hours to make. She messed up a few times with the X-Acto, almost ran out of cardstock. Out of a zip-lock bag she pulls out latex gloves and slips them on. With one hand, she holds the stencil against the permit sign, sprays with the other. Another dog barks, loud and deep. Someone slams a door. She stencils the bottom length of the entire application of development. Then she's done. She steps back and takes a look, holds up her phone, resists taking a photo.

I WANT CANDY

Après Afloat
Yaletown, Vancouver, BC
Open Thurs to Sun, 6 p.m.–2 a.m.

Review by: Jenny F.
Coal Harbour, Vancouver, BC
☆☆☆☆☆ November 16, 2082

I've been waiting for months to eat here, just to be in that rarefied air of a high-end lounge with impeccable food. Reservations pop up infrequently, but I'm persistent! Some girlfriends were in from out of town and through a series of fortunate coincidences (and connections—hi, Jimmy ♡!!) I got us a reservation here.

From the Parisian collegiate cottage-core decor to the wine list, it was love as soon as I sat down at the floating table. Micromolecular gastronomy is here and I felt my whole essence ensconced by the prosecco ventilator. And the protein foam! Breathe it in and feel your senses come alive! Every dish was better than the last, and the dessert was a drained gooseberry in edible soil coated in powdered sugar, flamed with a blowtorch. We each got one teaspoon, and the show of it all ... well, something to remember for a lifetime.

My girlfriends and I were offered premium vintage heroin in the powder room. Drug attendants are new, but I think will be all the rage in the next six months. It lives up to the hype!

And to know it was all only two hundred calories. A dream come true. Fed my soul!!

Review by: Nic B.
No known address
☆ November 16, 2082

Screech won't let you post a review with zero stars, which is pretty rude, if you ask me. And no one ever does. And if you've been reading my reviews, you know I've never eaten and never will at this fucking dump!

If you're rich enough to afford food that isn't government-issued rations, then you're tasting the flavours of the old gods. Me, I'm praying to the new gods (the vending machines in the bus depot) that the security guard gets severe butt-barfs so I can smash one of those things and get myself a whole row of Oh Henry!. I know there's peanuts in there, and that's protein. Can't believe people are still going out for dinner. Ha ha ha. It would be funny if it weren't so filthy.

Today I want to jump in with a review of the rations most people are eating these days. Not high-end raisin inhalers like Jenny F., but regular people. The masses.

So, the government claims the rations are "artisanal" and "seasonal" and "organic." Like that, you know, with the quotation marks that mean they're lying or whatever. Here is a transcript of a recent conversation between me and my bestie in our shared shipping container "condo":

ME: These rations look like baby poop and taste like cloth diapers.
BESTIE: Like, a diaper full of baby poop?
ME: No, they're so flavourless.
BESTIE: I bet the packaging is the baby poop smell. That wet synthetic cardboard is always a bit soggy, but the rations are bone dry.
ME: Exactly! Nailed it.
BESTIE: I think cloth diapers now are actually made out of recycled cardboard.
ME: That would explain the texture and flavour of these.

And ... scene.

So, yeah, I've never been to this bourgeois restaurant that has tables suspended from the goddamn ceiling like it's a production of *Peter Pan*. But I can say that it royally fucking sucks, it's bad, do not go there. Low rating. If I could give a rating lower than one star, I would—like underground-to-the-centre-of-the-Earth low.

Brunch Babe
Kitsilano, Vancouver, BC
Open Daily, 9 a.m.–3 p.m.

Review by: Jenny F.
Coal Harbour, Vancouver, BC
☆☆☆☆½ November 30, 2082

Ambience is at 100! This place has been on every top-ten brunch list for the past month. It's a very sensual space, filled with soft-pink lighting, and instead of tables there are perfectly made beds (silk sheets, of course, and napkins to match), and each bed is filled with the hottest people.

The unconventional cocktail choices are to die for, but I found the meal a bit too heavy. French toast mini crackers might seem like a great idea, but they were actually too filling! I couldn't even touch my ketamine-infused egg bite while soaking in the Ketamine Infusion After Pool. I was quite bloated!

Review by: Nic B.
No known address
☆ November 30, 2082

Do you know what's to die for? Literally most things, babe! Brunch, babe? Babe, are you brunching?

We're lucky out here if we can get a box of stale Cinnamon Toast Crunch at Christmas. Like, if someone donates it to the food bank and you happen to get there at exactly the right hour.

Saville's Sweets and Vape Shoppe
Mount Pleasant, Vancouver, BC
Open Daily, 10 a.m.–4 a.m.

Review by: Jenny F.
Coal Harbour, Vancouver, BC
☆☆☆½ December 3, 2082

I don't know what I ever did to Nic B., but I've reported those posts and I think they should be removed soon. I've heard that the Sunshine Shipping Container District is quite up-and-coming, so I hope Nic B. gets a better attitude! It's a privilege to live in an area with access to so many wonderful new hot spots and a view of the mountain on a day without severe rain or smoke!

But now, let's talk about something sweet and delicious! We did a four-course candy and vape pairing menu. Apparently, it's the only way to do it, so that's what we did! All the recommendations were correct, and it was a smash. The table's favourite was the Rosemary Honeysuckle Spider Slow-Release Soothers with the Web Cream Earl Grey Vape.

The servers, I have to say, were a bit rude, so despite the flavours, textures, and culinary mastery at Saville's Sweets, I had to lower this rating.

At one point, one of them asked us if we were finished, and clearly we were not! Any moron could see we were just chatting (a very interesting conversation about the new show *Ugly Baby Daycare*), so we still had an unused Flamingo Ringo Dingo vape cartridge. But this server assumed we had finished and tried to take it away. My friend almost slapped the server's hand, but I reminded her that service workers are people too! So, we decided my rating on Screech would be enough of a message to send to those working there.

Hopefully, next time they'll have a little more decorum to go with the tantalizing mouth feel!

Review by: Nic B.
No known address
☆ December 3, 2082

Jenny F. doesn't know I can barely remember what candy tastes like, but I know I fucking loved it. Why am I so mad? Take a guess. Take a wild guess. Do you know how many people I share a bathroom with? Fifteen. And it's not even in my shipping container block. I have to go down the ladder and into another compound. Could you do that, Jenny F.?

Jenny F. also doesn't know I staked out the dumpster behind Saville's Sweets and Vape Shoppe for over a week. And honestly, it was so worth it. I know people are paying top dollar for this, but if I had to rate the discards, I'd probably still give them a 100/10 stars! That bitch wasn't lying about the flavour or texture. Really good! Even after I had to scrape some vape juice off the giant lollies.

But back to my regularly scheduled program: Jenny F., I hate you! I hate you with every fibre of my high-sodium, trash-tasting, low-flavour diet! And yet, I dedicate this dumpster-diver saccharine feast to you and your phony ass.

I hope you choke on a vape cartridge!

You're a five-star piece of shit!

Nic B.'s posts have been removed.

Review by: Nic F.U.
No known address
☆☆☆ December 5, 2082

Hi everyone! I can start a new account every day. I don't have a job. This is basically my job! That's why I eat rations.

Just another reminder: I don't have a job and that is why I eat the rations!

EXTRA! EXTRA! I'm eating rations!

Oh yeah, and extra extra hate to Jenny F. and everyone like her. I hope instead of eating baby kitten intestines or whatever you're into, you eat a baby-shit smoothie. But please, don't make it a trend.

Nic F.U.'s posts have been removed.

Bongo Blaze Bar
Railtown, Vancouver, BC
Open Fri to Sun, 9 p.m.–5 a.m.

Review by: Jenny F.
Coal Harbour, Vancouver, BC
☆☆☆☆☆ December 10, 2082

First, I want to say I am devastated to hear of the tragic fire at the shipping container complex along the railyard.

I was at the Bongo Blaze Bar that night, in a turret room with friends. We had a clear view of the complex early in the evening (if 12 a.m. is early! LMAO) and then during the tragic fire. I have to say I did pass out briefly (it was just so relaxing!) and when I came to, my Himalayan salt lamp bong and jumbo flame EZ lighter had tumbled out of my hand, and I assume out the window. The fire was startling for everyone in the club.

I hope they find out who did this. I want to say I hope no one was hurt, but definitely someone was hurt. Multiple casualties. I am donating my bonus this quarter to a charity that provides temporary blanket rentals to those who are currently without homes: Hot Wool for the Houseless.

But I also want to say, WOW—this place really has everything! Private bongo rooms, bongs the size and shape of an adult giraffe, crystal candy dishes filled with handcrafted, locally sourced gummies, and the most beautiful silent servers! And no tips allowed here.

A true five-out-of-five experience! Couldn't rate this place higher. Ha ha ha! Higher. I've never felt more serene!

On her walk back to 4th Avenue, she passes houses, ones with single families and multiple floors and multiple bedrooms and multiple bathrooms, backyards, grass, and barbecues. At the end of the next block, she sees another developer's application permit posted in the ground. Platinum Corp again. She stops, pulls out the stencil, and sprays the sign. Gets three more signs in and has to open a new can. It's still early. She walks along the streets looking for signs. Finds them, pulls out the stencil. Five more times she sprays her sunny orange logo. A man comes out of his house as she's about to pull the cardstock out for a sixth spray. She thinks she hears him say "Hey!" and in shoving the stencil into her backpack, she tears the delicate middle section. She zips up her bag and runs until she gets to the cross street closest to the next express bus stop. The man probably wasn't talking to her at all, probably didn't even notice.

WORKING FOR THE WEEKEND

Paula slips into the hot springs' adults-only pool and sits with a hot jet stream of water pulsing into her back. She's planted herself in a shady patch. All the pools outside are in direct sunlight except for this one, which has a few shaded areas. It's the middle of June, not quite summer, but it's hot and will only get hotter—and drier. Next to her is a couple sitting close together, a scrawny man and a gorgeous woman. The man's wet hand propped on the woman's sunburned shoulder. Across the pool, a group of young men are roughhousing, chucking bottles of beer at each other and drunkenly slamming into everyone as they splash and kick. One of them, white and short with long hair, keeps screaming that he's "the fucking king!"

An older Chinese woman swims past in a floral one-piece and mutters, "Ugh, men," as she exits the pool and puts on a robe.

"Not all men," the scrawny man says to the beautiful woman he's with. His head is pressed to her shoulder.

"I know, babe," she says, reaching for his hand protectively.

Paula sighs and swims to the other side of the pool, away from the cuddling couple, back into the sunlight, pushing the concept of patriarchal structures as far from her mind as possible. This is supposed to be a getaway. But maybe she's being too judgmental. She doesn't know these people. Maybe the woman likes to keep the peace, maybe the scrawny man owns a nice car and she can't drive, maybe he has a great dick. None of those is a good enough reason to placate male fragility, though. Of course, not all men. It's just those particular men right there in the pool. They're the only ones in the world causing problems, now and throughout history. Please, point the blame at them.

Paula gets out of the water to check her phone. No new messages. She's not expecting her friends for a few hours, but they both said they'd try and get on the road earlier if they could. Mikey's kid had a dance performance, and Lisa had a meeting. Paula reminds herself that it's important to manage expectations, and they're not going to show up early just because she wants them to. They have lives.

This trip has been planned for months. Paula has had to change her vacation days three times now because of issues with Lisa's and Mikey's schedules. She's had to save up for a year on her hourly PetSmart wages to afford this. But it's fine, she's child-free and partner-free and her parents have both passed away, so it makes sense for her to be the one to make adjustments. And the three of them haven't been away together without children or partners in five years.

Their last trip was incredible. A friend of Mikey's had a seaside vacation house on one of the Gulf Islands and let them stay there for free. Cell service was bad. But the three of them smoked pot, drank cocktails, ate, cackled, and soaked in the hot tub.

The first night, while Paula was asleep, Mikey and Lisa stole her phone, went into her dating apps, and updated her profile. Mikey changed her photo to one she'd forced Paula to pose for that day, in her bikini and jorts. Lisa added to her description that Paula hated hikes—to keep out the outdoorsy types—and that her favourite movies were both scary and funny. Then the two of them took turns messaging people they thought she should hook up with or date, or just people they felt like harassing. When Paula woke up the next morning, there were messages from at least fifty women. Some were very flirty, some were kind, and some were furious.

"Did you have to say I love ogre porn?" Paula moaned. She was treating her hangover with a shot of tequila.

Lisa tried to grab Paula's phone again. "We didn't have to, but it was very fun to do."

"We had a system," Mikey said. "We only told every fifth person about ogre porn."

"This is what I get for telling you I watched that one Shrek and Fiona video. We're all curious, people!"

They went to the farmers' market to collectively select ingredients for meals, walked along the shoreline, created special cocktails for happy hour, and played crib on the patio. As the day turned to dusk, Lisa confessed that work was tiring and being high-powered was annoying. Mikey felt guilty for leaving her children behind but was beyond grateful for the break. Paula couldn't remember the last time she'd felt so happy.

"It really is so great being together," Lisa said.

"I miss this. I miss us being close. Like proximity-wise. A text isn't enough." Paula's voice cracked.

"No crying!" Mikey shouted. "I'm making Almost-Midnight Mai Tais and we're getting in the hot tub!"

With stars overhead, they sank into the hot tub, each of them sighing with relief and settling into comfortable silence.

"Next time we do this, there has to be a hot tub," Lisa said.

Mikey sat up suddenly, spraying Almost-Midnight Mai Tai on them as she spoke. "Hot springs!"

Paula laughed and nodded. "Just like our very first trip."

So they planned their twenty-fifth friendship anniversary trip for the same location where they'd first bonded during university, on a weekend away at the hot springs outside the city.

The older woman in the floral suit must have gone to complain about the aggressive men, because she comes back to the pool area accompanied by a small ginger woman in a blazer, name badge, and boxy skirt—a front-desk employee. The employee bends over the edge of the pool, waving her arms to get the guys' attention. Sitting in a deck chair, Paula can't hear the conversation, but the employee seems to be scolding them. The guys reluctantly get out of the pool, tossing their empty bottles into the garbage can beside the recycling bin. The Fucking King sees the older woman coming around the other side of the pool, near Paula. He tosses a tall-boy can to the ground.

"Fuck you, bitch! We're just having fun."

"This place is haunted, look at that goddamn ghoul!" says his friend.

"I ain't afraid of no ghost!" says the Fucking King.

The woman waves in their direction, rotating her hand at the wrist like the Queen.

"Please leave now," the employee says. "You're banned from the pool for today." She gestures for them to move along, so polite as she bends down to pick up the cans they've left behind and drop them into the recycling bin. The group shouts and whoops as they enter the hotel through a side door. Following them, the employee nods at the woman, who removes her robe, adjusts her hat, and takes a chair beside the pool.

"I'm sorry. They're awful," Paula says to her.

"I'm seventy-three, I've seen shitheads like that my whole life. I don't have patience for them anymore. How old are you?"

"I'm forty-two."

"You shouldn't have time for that either."

"Yeah, I don't really. Thank you for dealing with that. I should have said something too."

"Ah, we all get tired sometimes."

"That's true. Last time I was here I felt odd. Like a little off. Now, too. Maybe it's all the relaxation. Or maybe the vibes are off. I know there are all sorts of rumours about this place."

"Yes, there are plenty of rumours. The waters here are supposed to be powerful. Very healing."

"I heard the hotel itself has a lot of history."

"Well, it *is* haunted. I've been here enough times to know. Ghosts. Demons. Evil. Once I saw an old woman jump from a four-storey window, and there was nothing on the ground afterward."

"That's horrific!"

"I know. I still love to come here, though. Getting in the water. All the different temperatures. Where's your room? The fancy new renovated section, or the old wing up there?"

"It's in the old wing."

"Oh. I always ask not to stay there."

"Is the plumbing bad or something?"

"No, a man killed his wife there sixty years ago. They say you can hear her complaining up and down the old wing between the solstice and the equinox. She caught him cheating, and he drowned her in the bathtub. I heard her once. Groaning in the night. Never went there again."

Paula looks up in the direction of her room. It had seemed innocuous enough. Old, but innocuous.

"Well, thanks for telling me. And thanks for getting those guys out of here."

"Fuck those little shits. I hope a poltergeist crawls into their assholes at night." The woman drops her saucer-sized sunglasses onto her face and leans back in the lounger.

"You're a badass!"

Paula doesn't have patience for shitheads either, but she didn't want them to yell at her for yelling at them. She picks up her towel and puts on her hotel-provided robe, dropping her phone into the pocket. On her way inside, she glances back at the older woman basking in the sun, looking glorious.

Before heading back to her room, Paula stops by the spa on the main level.

"Can I book some treatments? It's for three people."

She's saved up for spa treatments for them all. A treat. She hasn't had a manicure in years, though she knows her friends get them regularly.

"Let me check the schedule," the employee says.

They're here for four days, and aside from one meal reservation, they're pretty much clear to do anything they like. Paula has been dreaming of spending time together for months. Just being able to chat for hours with her friends will fill her cup. Everyone has been so busy, and she's starting to worry that a few days away every few years might be the only time she gets to enjoy Lisa's and Mikey's company now. They've been friends for twenty-five years, but the past few have been a slowly lengthening dry spell of cancelled hangouts, dinners, and outings, building to a drought of nothing ever working out and no one ever seeing each other. The last-minute cancellations feel the worst, usually after she's spent time showering and primping as if for a date—back when dating was remotely interesting. But her friends are important. Why not dress up for them? Even if they'd just be sitting in a dark movie theatre.

The spa employee clicks away at her tablet. "I've got appointments for three either this evening, tomorrow morning, or early afternoon the day after."

"Perfect, I'll take the morning appointments tomorrow. The Pre-Pool Pamper. Girls' trip!" Paula waves her hands above her head and laughs. The spa employee doesn't react.

"Okay, we'll see the three of you then."

Paula turns and nearly collides with a white woman about twenty years older than her. She's dressed in red florals with a caftan, and there's a glow about her.

"Oh, sorry."

The woman says nothing, just eyes Paula up and down with a bemused smile before staring into her face. Intensely. Maybe that's what aging is good for: intensity.

"Excuse me, ma'am, you forgot your room key!" the spa employee says.

Paula goes back to grab her key card. When she leaves the spa, the woman in red is gone.

She heads to her room to kill some more time and clean herself up a little. Flinging open the door, she walks abruptly into the wooden suitcase stand and barks her shins, forgetting that she'd moved things around and shut the blinds.

"Shit!"

She yelps and fumbles to turn on a light. This wing of the hotel hasn't been updated in many years. The bed frame looks vintage, and the room is small. There's a tiny step to get into the bathroom, which has a tiny shower, a separate tiny bathtub, and barely enough room to turn around between the two. The lighting is poor—a single dim light on the ceiling and a small bedside lamp. Thick blinds hang over the only window in the main room, which looks out onto a strange corner of the old building, with a sliver view of the mountains and the pool below. Just off from the pool is the old restaurant, the Copper Room, which she can see into from the bathroom window above the bathtub. It's been there for 150 years, still operating even though they've built new cafés and brunch bars and slushie bar extensions. A historical space with dim overhead lighting and tall candlesticks at every table, like they want you to host a seance.

Her hotel suite reminds her of the many apartments in the city she's lived in over the years. Kept up just enough to justify the maximum rent increase per year, too small to be perfectly comfortable, but somehow, there was always some feature that endeared her. This strange bathroom with a tub and a separate shower is that for this hotel room. She can wash off the chlorine and then soak again if she wants to.

Paula soaps off the pool water, washes her hair, and dries it with the tiny hair dryer attached to the wall. She pulls on the second robe—for guests who might be staying with a second person—and does her makeup. Being here alone means double the towels, double the robes, and double the toiletries, and she plans to use them all. Her wet swimsuit hangs to dry over the shower door. Water droplets splashing onto the tile floor echo in the tiny bathroom.

Since there's still time to kill, she fills the tub and drops in a bath bomb, gets her book, and slides into the foamy water that smells of rosemary and strawberries. Orange-and-fuchsia light filters in through the bathroom blinds. The sound of her swimsuit dripping is rhythmic, almost mesmerizing.

The sound seems to be getting louder—then she realizes they're footsteps, cadent thumps drawing closer. Suddenly, someone's fingers are tight around her throat, and her head is pushed underwater. Her screams pierce her own ears, and all she can see is red streaks on the surface of the water above her.

She wakes abruptly, panting, her hands around her neck, her legs thrashing the water. She's splashed it everywhere. The bathwater is still frothy pink but cold now, and her chest feels heavy, tight. That one pina colada really knocked her out. Her new friend at the pool must really have gotten under her skin with all that ghost talk. She starts to shiver a little.

After getting out and drying off, then mopping up all the spilled bathwater, she slips into her second swimsuit and tosses on a colourful caftan over it, adding the chunky necklace Mikey gave her a few birthdays ago and the earrings Lisa brought her from Mexico. Paula's thrifted straw purse and her strappy flat sandals are the perfect accompaniments. She looks like a long-haired Mrs. Roper, and she likes it. A very old TV character kept alive all these years later by annual pub crawls in her honour, with folks wearing loose dresses, bright orange wigs, and strands of large baubles around their necks as they hop from bar to bar. In their late twenties, Paula, Mikey, and Lisa went on these pub crawls for a few years in a row, back when they thought turning twenty-nine was getting old.

Paula slips on her sunglasses, grabs her key, and leaves her room again. It's happy hour, and she still has an hour or more to wait. Walking down the hall, she spots the rowdy dudes from earlier huddled outside the elevator.

"We got banned from the pool, remember?"

"But I'm already bored. Let's just go back in."

"Don't be an idiot. We'll wait until that bitch from the front desk is gone. No one else will recognize us."

"Let's go down to the pub. Get some burgers and beers and be back here for nighttime in the *adults-only* pool."

They all laugh. The Fucking King punches a tall guy in a backward baseball hat. The backward hat guy punches him back. Then they all get into the elevator together.

"Hey, that lady wants to come in. Don't be shy."

The Fucking King smiles at Paula as the rest continue punching each other. Paula makes a show of rummaging through her nearly empty bag.

"Oh, I forgot something. Go on without me."

And then the door is closed and they're gone. She waits a few seconds, pushes the down button. Her phone beeps. A photo from

Lisa. She's standing in front of a billboard for the goat farm about fifty kilometres away. Her blond hair is pulled into a ponytail, and she's holding up a huge bottle of vodka, with her leg kicked out behind her. She and Mikey must have decided to travel together, because clearly the photo was taken by someone else standing far away. Unless she asked a stranger, which doesn't seem like Lisa, letting someone she doesn't know touch her phone. She's such a germophobe. Mikey doesn't give a shit, though. She'd lick a porta-potty on a dare.

Paula texts back the selfie she took earlier: she in her sunglasses and one-piece with a pina colada before the bros descended on the pool. The light was perfect, a sunburst behind her. Lisa sends a heart reaction.

Paula and Mikey have known Lisa's husband, Dave, as long as Lisa has. They were all at university together. When they started dating, he understood that she and her friends were a package deal. If he came over to their dorm, he had to bring them each a brownie from the caf, or Lisa would yell at him that he was getting dumped.

They dated for fifteen years, even though Lisa had always said living with a man sounded terrible. Sometimes she questioned what she was doing with Dave.

"I need my own space and my own bank account and everything."

"You make him share with us all the time," Mikey said.

"That's his job! To share with women."

"And you always share with us," Paula said.

"It's everyone's job to share with women!" Lisa shouted.

But she didn't want to break up with him. She loved him way too much, was way too obsessed with his long curly hair and his great attitude.

Dave was a romantic who wanted a wife and a big wedding, so he finally proposed, to which Lisa said, "Maybe. I don't know. I have to go."

She fled the fancy condo in the city she'd been planning to sell to live with Dave in the burbs and went to Paula's one-bedroom walk-up. Mikey came over too, heavily pregnant. All three of their phones buzzed and rang continuously with messages and calls from Dave, who was trying desperately to find Lisa—a musical accompaniment to her panicked sobs.

"I don't want to lose myself," she sobbed, sitting in Paula's bathtub.

They coaxed her out of the bathtub with pad Thai and spring rolls. Using the couch cushions and all of Paula's blankets, they built a cozy fort on the living room rug. Lisa nestled in, Paula cradling her. Mikey sat in the armchair.

"We love Dave," she said.

"And neither of us likes men that much," Paula added.

"It's kind of ideal. This way we don't have to talk about your spouse behind your back, like our other friends do."

"We love you. And Dave loves you, and you are so in love with Dave. It's kind of sickening. It makes me barf sometimes," Paula said.

"Shut the hell up, you guys."

Lisa calmed down, and she called Dave back, and everyone cried, and they got married.

In the hotel bar, the oddly low seating area is full, but no one is sitting at the actual bar. Paula orders a nine-ounce glass of rosé and a tiny bowl of half-priced olives, both of which the bartender brings over quickly. This is the advantage of sitting at the bar. She clicks through her phone. No new messages. No emails. No social media notifications. A saved article about allegations of fraud around a popular raw pet food brand. She's on vacation. She doesn't need to be reading that. Instead, she searches for information about the hotel—maybe some history or horror nerd has a made a podcast about it. After scrolling for ten minutes, she settles on a website run by an archivist and a journalist, two friends who share an interest in research and the paranormal. The first resort at this location was built in 1886. It burned down in 1920, was rebuilt in 1926, and then was expanded and renovated many times since.

She scrolls through, looking for any mentions of the woman who jumped out the window and the murdered woman. Yes, they're there, along with an old couple who had their throats slashed by a drifter. Their bloody bodies were found in bed, and ever since, people have claimed to see bloody footprints in that hallway. There's a comment section where resort guests are encouraged to report their own supernatural experiences. Paula skims the stories, which have all occurred in the old wing, where she's staying. It makes her shiver.

"What are you reading?"

Paula looks up. The woman in red from the spa is sitting beside her. Paula hadn't noticed her sitting down, even though the woman is so close she's almost touching Paula.

"How do you know I'm not playing Donut Blast?"

"You had a look of deep concentration and fascination. I'm Joanie, by the way."

"I'm Paula. Nice to meet you." Paula holds up her glass, and Joanie clinks her own against it. "I'm reading about the history of the resort. The creepier aspects."

"Oh, of course. Some people come here just for the ghosts, not the hot springs."

"I can believe it. The stories are pretty gnarly. I should probably stop reading them. I already had a nightmare today while I was in the bathtub. I woke up choking myself!" Paula laughs, mining the choking, and Joanie cackles along.

"The stories are getting to you."

"I didn't realize cleanliness could be such a hazard." Paula takes a sip of wine. "I guess I was too relaxed."

"Nothing like a nightmare to shake you up. They can be motivating. A real adrenalin rush."

Paula looks at her phone for the time and flips on the camera to check her lipstick.

"You look fabulous, love," Joanie says. "Are you meeting up with someone special?"

"No—I mean, yes. My friends."

"Friends, huh."

"Yeah. Maintaining friendships is really important as one gets older, don't you think?"

Joanie doesn't respond except to suck up the rest of her pink cocktail through her straw.

"You here for business?" Paula asks.

"No, I'm all by myself. Until now!" Joanie smiles. "So, where are your friends, then?"

Paula's phone beeps. It's Mikey saying they'll be there in half an hour. Paula guzzles the rest of her wine and, feeling a little buzz, holds up her phone to show Joanie the photo of herself with Mikey and Lisa on her lock screen.

"They'll be here soon. Getting together has been a long time coming. They have such busy lives, and it took me so much planning. But it's finally our big girls' trip!"

"Sounds like you have to accommodate them a lot."

"No, it's not like that."

"And they're driving together? Without you?"

"Yeah, it's okay, I like to get on the road early. Plus they had other commitments beforehand—family and stuff."

"You don't have any family?"

"Nope, it's just me. That's why my friends are so important."

Joanie reaches out a bangled arm and squeezes it around Paula's shoulders. She smells like campfire ash, which Paula likes. Joanie grips Paula's chin in her manicured fingertips and smiles at her, making deep eye contact. "Honey, you are so lovely. I'm having a good time! I want to know everything about you."

"Well, a very glamorous woman did tell me I look fabulous!"

Paula nods at the bartender, and he brings her another glass of wine. She takes a sip and shoves some olives into her mouth, glad to have them, as she hasn't eaten since this morning. When she looks up, there's another pink concoction in Joanie's hand.

"What is that you're drinking? It looks so fun."

Holding the glass above her head, Joanie swishes her drink without spilling a drop, then lowers it to her red lips and takes a delicate sip, leaving no trace of lipstick on the rim.

"This here is my own invention. It's all I drink. I came up with it ages ago, and the bartender made it for me. Gin, ginger beer, strawberries, raspberries, and a special little liqueur that's quite uncommon. I call it Too Much Blush. Even though I don't believe anyone can wear too much blush. It's to die for!"

"It looks very enticing."

"You're very enticing! An independent woman doing your own thing. Reading ghost stories and getting tipsy with strangers. Enjoying olives. Flouncing about."

Laughing, Paula leans back and feels like she might flip right over. "Oof, I *am* getting a little tipsy. I think I'll head outside, maybe absorb some of that healing water to clear my head. Care to join me?"

"Oh, I never go in the water. Not for me."

"It can get a little wild out there. Even in the middle of the afternoon."

"Well, enjoy your friends," Joanie says. "I hope you have a good time. You deserve a good time. Though it's strange they didn't travel up with you." She snorts a laugh and raises her glass to Paula.

Paula raises her own and drains the rest of her wine. When she's finished, she finds that her caftan buddy has disappeared.

The two glasses of wine have made her more light-headed than usual, as if she's had double the amount of alcohol. She goes outside and asks the poolside bartender to fill her water bottle, drains it, then asks for the same again before ordering three small bags of potato chips. She sets up near the lap pool, away from the adults-only area for now and closer to the bar. From there she can see several tall fir trees and, behind them, the parking lot. She cracks into her first bag of chips, sour cream and onion, and slams them. Little crumbs fill her cleavage. She checks her phone. It's 4 p.m. They should be here by now. She texts them her exact location.

She takes out the self-help book she's trying to read, *Living Alone and Loving Every Ever-Loving Living Minute of It*. Every time she starts a new sentence, she starts to doze, so finally she gives in to it. Her brain swirls with images from all the stories on the website. A woman jumping out a window into a decorative bush. The dead bodies of the elderly couple. And then she sees herself but not herself, a version of her, eyes red, hair sparked out around her head like she's being electrocuted, hands grabbing the side of the pool with enough strength to crack the concrete. The whole surface of the Earth moves at her touch.

She wakes a moment later to find a server standing over her with a tray. On it sits a pink cocktail in a plastic cup. "You ordered this inside." He sets it on the metal table beside her chair.

Paula looks back and sees Joanie waving at her from the entrance to the pool area. She waves back and holds up the drink, then closes her eyes and takes a sip. It tastes good, refreshing. But after a few more sips, she feels heat rising up her throat, like someone has lit a match in her esophagus. Must be the ginger beer.

Joanie is nowhere to be seen now, but a herd of humans whose voices she recognizes walk onto the sunlit pool deck, making her drop her cocktail. It pools pink around her flip-flops.

"Hi, Paula!" Lisa says.

"Surprise!" Mikey shouts, waving her wide-brimmed straw hat.

Beside Mikey are her two children. Behind Lisa stands her husband, Dave, pulling a rolling suitcase, a white streak of zinc across his nose. Everyone is smiling broadly, expectantly.

"Sorry we're late. Both kids got diarrhea."

"We did a caravan! So we also stopped when they got diarrhea."

What the fuck is this? They brought their families on our special trip? Paula's head is swimming in booze and something else that feels like a burning chemical ooze sloshing behind her eyeballs, coupled with the searing sensation in her throat that's reached her mouth. She feels like she could puke flames. She drops her head forward and rolls it back, then snaps upright, perfectly straight, staring at her friends. The fire behind her eyes is now spreading to her entire body.

She stands up, placing her foot directly in the cold, sugary slush and barely noticing a tiny hiss of steam rising. She puts her caftan back on and takes a step toward them without a word. Everyone is staring at her.

Lisa drops her travel tote to the ground. "Paula, what's wrong?"

There's a strong buzzing in Paula's head. The drinks. The woman who thought she was fabulous. The melted pink slush she stepped in. Her entire body is on fire. For a brief moment she thought things were perfect, but that illusion's gone. She feels like her cropped nails could scratch a slip of skin off someone if they said the wrong thing to her. Her own skin tingles.

"Why are *they* all here?" she asks Mikey and Lisa.

"We're on vacation?" Mikey says.

Paula balls her hands into fists at her sides.

"Yes, we're all here. Just look at the trees, the hot springs, the mountains, the fresh air. This is the perfect weather. Let's enjoy it!" Lisa adds.

"I *was* enjoying myself. Lounging, drinking, soaking," Paula says. She reaches into her swimsuit and flicks chip crumbs out of her cleavage. Some of them land in Lisa's son's hair.

"That's rude," Lisa says.

"Is it not rude to invite other people on a girls' trip without asking?"

Oblivious to the tension, Mikey's kids take off running around the pool deck, shouting each other's names as loudly as possible, "Jetta!" and "Kiki!," "Jetta!" and "Kiki!," over and over again. Paula flicks the last of her cleavage crumbs onto the ground. Dave stares at her as if he's never met her.

"I don't think we ever discussed this as a girls' trip. Did we?" Mikey asks.

"Dave has time off right now," Lisa says.

"Oh, does he? Good for Dave."

Mikey goes to round up her kids like a herd dog. Hunched over, she chases them around the lap pool. Lisa and Dave form a blockade when they run back around.

"Okay, stop running now! I mean it!" Mikey grabs the necks of her children's T-shirts like the scruff of a cat's neck. "Paula, we're sorry, but can't you be more accommodating?"

"More accommodating? I am the most accommodating person you've ever met. Look at me accommodate. I just wish someone had told me it was a family reunion. What a joy! Just what I wanted!" Paula retorts.

Her entire field of vision is red, and every cell of her skin seethes with rage. She stares at her friends again—they look so confused, concerned. Why *is* she reacting like this? She whips off her caftan and dives into the pool, swims the length underwater, screaming "Fuck!" the entire time. The bubbles coming out of her mouth look tinged with blood. Maybe it's food colouring from the Too Much Blush.

When she emerges, her friends are gone, but a waiting hotel employee points at a "NO DIVING" sign. "First warning is final warning. If you do it again, you're banned!" he says.

Paula crawls out of the pool, gasping for air. "Sorry, I didn't even know what I was doing."

She's never flipped out on anyone before, let alone Mikey and Lisa. They looked scared of her. It was like her body and mind unhinged themselves. Aging has made her change in all sorts of ways—like having the one stinky armpit and waking up at 3 a.m. every night—but uncontrolled rage hasn't been on the menu so far.

Embarrassed, she goes back to the lounge chair, wipes up her spilled drink, and wraps a towel around herself. Time to dry off and dry out for the day.

When Mikey told them she was planning to have kids as a single parent, they weren't shocked—she'd always wanted them—but they were worried. Sure, she had a good job with excellent benefits, she owned her home, and she had all sorts of supportive people in her life. With her tallness and her severe black bob, she looked like she could dominate any situation. But raising kids alone was a lot.

"It won't be alone, I've got people."

"Oh, we know," Paula said.

"I'm gonna do it."

"We know!" Paula said again.

"I'm ready for cute Filipino babies! And as soon as possible. I'm doing it as soon as possible."

"We figured," Lisa said.

Two years later, Lisa invited them over for a weekend visit to sort out Mikey's birth plan and the first few weeks of her first kid's life. Lasagna bubbled in the oven while they all pored over calendars and checklists. Paula compiled a meal train as she drained a box of Pinot grigio. Sipping a spritzer, Lisa set up a group chat with everyone who could possibly be called on for assistance. Mikey chomped on chunks of Parmesan the whole time. She was weirdly superstitious of baby showers or any other gatherings or celebrations before the baby was born, so instead, Paula organized a helper visitation sheet, with each person assigned to bring Mikey an item from a carefully curated registry.

When Mikey's water broke, Lisa and Paula rushed over, got her to the hospital, and stayed with her through the eleven hours of labour and the emergency C-section. They booked time off work to take turns staying at Mikey's during the first few weeks, Paula taking transit for two hours to get to her (she didn't have a car back then) and Lisa driving in from a different suburb. Sometimes all three of them were there at the same time, which made it easier and also more fun. The baby had both *Lisa* and *Paula* as middle names.

"Kiki Lisa Paula. I thought, hey, she needs as many vowels as possible," Mikey said.

Paula cradled that baby like it was her own.

Too mortified to respond to any of Lisa's and Mikey's two dozen messages, back in her room, Paula looks at herself in the bathroom mirror. Her face is streaked in makeup. She wasn't supposed to get her face wet after applying foundation and mascara (not waterproof), but she was too angry in the moment to remember that she wanted to look nice. Now she sees what a monster she was. How humiliating.

It's so like her to be kind of a fuck-up. To spend all this time planning and then act like a loser. She registers for fitness classes and signs up for lesbian swimming club at the aquatic centre, but never exercises. Her discount produce delivery comes on Tuesdays, she makes one full-hearted attempt at a meal, and then it goes mostly rotten by Sunday. On Saturday afternoons she sits in a nest of salty snacks and watches old music videos until she drifts off into a nap. Her life, her job—they're not that great. Maybe she isn't, either. She feels both guilty and betrayed. They showed up with their families without warning or explanation, taking her for granted, again. All they had to do was talk to her beforehand and let her know the situation. She loves Dave and Mikey's kids, but that doesn't mean she wants to spend this vacation with them. Is she not allowed to have complicated feelings? Maybe she is, but she needs to be less aggressive in communicating them. That's what Mikey says to her kids.

Lisa was right. It's the perfect weather, almost like when they were young, and bad wildfires only came every second year or so. Of course they wanted their loved ones to enjoy themselves too. Dave is great with the kids and will surely hang out with them while the three of them go to the spa or sit in the adults-only pool looking at the stars. Maybe it'll all be fine. Even if they're mad at her, she can apologize. She hasn't even told them about the spa appointment yet. She has that up her sleeve.

She gulps down a blue Gatorade, orders a pizza, and eats it while sitting in her wet swimsuit in the empty bathtub, watching people below go in and out of the old restaurant. It reminds her of the Overlook Hotel in *The Shining*—all six movie adaptations were filmed in the creepiest hotels. It's dark and fancy looking but also old and creepy, like it's draped in velvet. She swigs from her water bottle, trying to rehydrate. She's shed some tears, and her face is salty.

An old couple, both with canes, help each other out of the restaurant and into the evening air. It's a week away from summer solstice, and the sky gets darker here than in the city. The mountains lock the sun down earlier. Joanie comes walking past the old couple. Leaning closer to the window to get a better look, Paula sees Joanie looking up at her before cackling and shaking her head back and forth. Then she's gone from Paula's sight. Or her vision. Maybe she's still drunk. She slinks back down, below the window, and finishes her pizza, the box lying on her chest.

Her phone keeps sounding with notifications, which she ignores. They don't know what room she's in. Her swimsuit's dry now, so she decides to go back for one more dip before the pool closes for the night. She swipes at her face with makeup wipes, then reapplies a small amount of eyeshadow and mascara, eyeliner and a bold berry lip. She puts her caftan back on and throws her hair into a bun, then finishes a second Gatorade in a long chug.

What got into her? If it was too much alcohol, she can easily avoid doing that again. She's eaten a whole pizza, had time to rest, and flossed her teeth too. After a relaxing soak, she'll feel ready to apologize and spend time with Mikey and Lisa, if they want to see her.

The bros are back by the elevator. They've got a Coleman cooler with them, and the Fucking King is sitting on it. This time they're quiet, probably trying to be inconspicuous. At least for now. When the elevator comes, they let her enter first.

"Ma'am, would you like a seat?" one of them says, indicating the cooler.

She shakes her head as they all laugh. She's trapped behind them.

"If anyone tries to fuck up our night, I will crush them."

"Maybe we just chill for once."

"Yeah, we've already been partying pretty hard."

The Fucking King is not interested in this. "Don't be fucking pussies."

"Sorry, ma'am. We think pussies are great."

Thankfully, the elevator opens, and they all get out. As the bros loudly disperse, Paula spots Joanie in the lobby.

"Hello, again. How are your friends?"

"Um, I kind of blew up at them."

"Oh really?" Joanie presses a loose bobby pin back into her hair.

"Yeah, they brought, like, their entire families with them. So, it's not really a girls' trip now. But it's fine. It's not a big deal. I don't know why I lashed out."

"Of course you do. Sometimes we have to speak our truth. And anger can be your greatest friend. Good for you."

Paula shakes her head. "I'm not usually like that. It was intense. Maybe I drank too much."

"Nah. No such thing."

Joanie is looking at her strangely, staring into her eyes again. Maybe she's been hitting on Paula this whole time.

"I like that we both like caftans," Paula says.

"Me too. I like to be comfortable. So, how did you like my drink?"

"It was so good. Sweet but intense. Interesting aftertaste. I didn't get to finish it, though."

"It's powerful. Fierce. Just like we are, love."

"Mom! I hate it here!" A small child races in on a scooter, slamming to a stop right beside Paula and almost crashing into Joanie, as if he hasn't even noticed her. Joanie steps back to make room. "I want to see a real bear!" the boy says to his mother, who's racing after him. "The kind of bear that rips off the head of a rabbit! Like in the book!"

"What book?!" the mother asks.

Joanie turns back to Paula. "Well, if you need the complaints department, I'll be down here later." She points toward the bar with a shiny black-lacquered finger and winks. "Too Much Blushes are on me!"

The mother and child, still arguing about headless rabbits and vicious bears, get into the elevator, and Joanie steps in after them, nodding at Paula.

Paula soaks in the adults-only pool for an hour. The water is warm and the air is warm, and she is hydrated and alone and fine. The bros are remarkably calm in their spot in the pool. They're swearing and high-fiving, but nothing sinister. Even the Fucking King is saying sorry when he bumps into someone.

Then Paula spots Lisa and Mikey on the wooden walkway above the bros. Time to apologize. Time to explain that she overreacted because she had a pina colada and two glasses of wine and a few sips of a Too Much Blush and only ate some olives and chips.

They spot her too. As they approach, she hops out of the pool to meet them, drying herself off. But the closer her friends get, the closer she feels her eyebrows drawing toward each other. A burning tingle rises in her, and from ankles to forehead, she's feels as if she's aflame. Like she could spit burning venom and end them. She looks up at the hotel in some kind of desperation. Here she is, a pathetic adult hanging out alone, when she's supposed to be spending quality time with her closest friends. Her neck lolls on her shoulders again, boiling steam building inside her.

Maybe Joanie was right. She's allowed to have feelings and express them. She grabs her things in a messy pile. She wants to head inside the hotel, but Lisa and Mikey each take a side, trying to corner her. Paula jumps back into the pool, holding her things above her head, the hem of the caftan dangling in the water. Her friends are looking at her like she's an animal. She's behaving horribly again. She has to get out of this.

Lisa and Mikey position themselves, one each, at the ladders on either end of the pool and then get in, moving toward her from both sides. When Paula gets to the far end with the bros, she's stuck with nowhere to go but up onto the walkway, but she can't reach it. She feels embarrassed.

"Give me a boost!" she says to the Fucking King.

"What, ma'am?"

"Are you okay, Paula?" Lisa calls out. "Take a moment to breathe."

"Are those people harassing you? Because that's not cool," the Fucking King says.

"If you're the Fucking King, get me out of here right the fuck now!" Paula says, pointing up at the walkway.

The Fucking King puts out his clasped hands. Paula steps into them and hauls herself up and over the railing of the walkway.

"Come on, Paula! Don't be so immature!" Lisa yells.

"I'm not immature, you are! You guys can't do anything on your own."

"You're being a jackass!" Mikey shouts.

Paula makes her way back inside the hotel, but Mikey runs in from another door and accosts her near the fireplace. It's hot—Paula feels like flames are coming out of her cheeks.

"What's gotten into you?" Mikey says as Lisa comes around the corner. Sighing, Paula relents, leaning against a pillar, her head down.

"Paula," Lisa says. "We are so happy to see you."

"Are you really?"

"What kind of question is that?" Mikey asks.

"Your eyes look, like, really bloodshot or something. They're so red. Are you allergic to the pool chemicals?"

The little kid from earlier rolls up on his scooter. He stops and glares at Paula, then pulls out a plastic water cannon and shoots her right in the face.

"Oh my God!" Paula splutters.

Then comes a body shot, and then he's scooting out of there. The water is warm. The kid must have filled his gun with pool water.

"What the hell, kid," Lisa mutters.

Paula wipes her face with her caftan. She looks at her friends, again showing concern and confusion. Her hands are shaking, and she wants to run away. It's as if she's having a bad dream. Tears start streaming down her face, and Mikey and Lisa embrace her.

"I'm sorry, guys. I dunno what's going on with me."

"I didn't realize you would be so upset if we brought Dave and the kids," Lisa says.

"Come on, we'll still spend time together," Mikey adds.

"Of course we will. We just got here."

"No, I get it. I shouldn't be acting this way," Paula says. "I just don't feel like myself. But, um, I booked us for mani-pedis in the morning. My treat."

"Oh, that's great!"

Lisa holds up her hands to show them her freshly gelled nails. "I'll just get a pedi, but I love it."

A spark of irritation blooms in Paula's chest. It's just a manicure. But it's also another rejection. She slams her back against the pillar and slinks down to the floor, takes her hair out of the bun and shakes it out.

"Let's go for a soak. It'll make us all relax," Lisa says.

Mikey checks her phone. "I don't have much time. I gotta put the kids to bed soon."

Paula grits her teeth. She'd rather leave than snap again. But her feet feel like lead, as if she's fighting her own instinct to get away. "Okay, put the kids to bed," she says. "I'll go pull myself together. I gotta properly take off all this makeup."

"Let's meet out at the pool in like an hour. Just us. I'll make Dave stay with the kids. He likes to be with his iPad anyway," Lisa says.

Paula goes upstairs and swipes her face with micellar water, brushes her hair back into a bun, and throws her caftan back on. The single light above her flickers. She grabs her bag and goes back down to the lobby. She's already feeling unhinged—why stay here and be creeped out?

She exits the hotel to stroll along the beach, passing people laughing together, sitting on the sand with ice creams and secret bottles of beer. Her friends want her to be happy for them, to share in their lives. But maybe she's not happy for them all the time. That's not what she wanted this weekend to be about.

Five years ago Paula had a health crisis. She had been feeling rough, and then a test came back, and it wasn't good, so she had to have more tests. And more tests. Her doctor said the only way to figure out what was going on was a hospital procedure where they put you under and cut you open and send a tiny floating camera to roam around inside your body, looking for small masses and cancerous cells.

Paula video-called Lisa and Mikey, and miraculously, they both answered. "Hey, guys, fun news. I'm getting a somewhat invasive cancer screening."

Lisa gasped. "What?"

"Excuse you—cancer?" Mikey said.

Paula had been keeping her health problems to herself for weeks, letting it roll around inside her, just like the cancer that might be clinging to her stomach. Why worry her friends if it wasn't anything serious?

"I have to get a procedure."

"Whenever it is, we'll be there."

"Of course we will! Whatever you need. I'm gonna clear my schedule."

She hated being an emotional burden. She twisted her hands against her abdomen while Mikey talked about medical advancements and Lisa smiled, though she clearly wanted to cry, which made Paula want to cry too. Her head was cloudy, but she sent them the details. It wouldn't be for a few weeks. Everyone had time to prepare. Though Paula had never felt so unprepared.

Lisa and Mikey weren't able to fully clear their schedules but said they'd be at the hospital an hour before Paula was scheduled to come out of anaesthesia. Dr. Sharma was tall and beautiful and kept telling Paula it was all going to be easy and breezy. Nurses swept in and out of the room while she lay on the bed, staring at the ceiling. The doctor asked if Paula wanted to see the little robot, and she did. It was so small and so cute; it didn't look like something that was going to do serious medical service. Then a nurse covered her face with a mask and she heard gas and then nothing.

Three hours later, she woke up to see her beautiful doctor standing at the window, illuminated by sunlight. For a moment, she wasn't sure if she was alive or dead.

"Hello Paula, I hope you're feeling all right," Dr. Sharma said.

"I feel okay, I guess."

"I can give you the good news right away: We didn't find any cancer. The bad news is that your intestines are not happy, but they're not going to kill you. I've got a treatment plan for IBS for you. I'll explain it when you're less groggy and email you a copy too."

"Thank you."

Paula tried to sit up, but her body had other ideas. She slumped back against the pillows.

"You'll need to rest for a while longer. Do you have anyone coming to pick you up? You're supposed to be released to someone who will get you home and look after you."

"Oh yeah, my friends are coming. I just need to check my phone."

There were messages: They were on their way. They were stopping for coffee and croissants. They were running a quick errand. They would be there soon. There was an accident on the bridge. The bridge was shut down. No one could get through. They weren't coming. They were turning around and going back home. They were sorry. They should have left sooner.

"I'm glad you don't have cancer," Lisa said on their video call that night.

"Me too," Mikey said.

"Me three. I really didn't want it." Paula laughed, making light of things.

She wanted to end the call but stayed on while they talked about a reality show she hated. She wanted to hang up dramatically and go sit in the bathtub with a growler of IPA. She wanted to tell them she was hurt and a bit angry and tired of feeling like her needs meant nothing. But instead, she listened to them talk about this VR dating show where the contestants had to guess whether they were dating a robot, a real person, or a parrot. Paula had once considered getting a parrot, but they lived a long time, and she had no one to leave it to when she died.

"Well, I gotta go, guys! I don't have cancer, but IBS calls."

The bar is still open. Walking through, she sees her badass friend from the pool, the one who dealt with the bros. She's sitting in a low, comfy chair by the window, looking out into the beautiful evening light. Her round black sunglasses are perched in her perfectly white hair.

"Hi, remember me?"

"Hello, yes."

"Sorry, I'm Paula. I should have introduced myself before."

"Everyone calls me Sal."

"Good to see you again. I hope you've been able to relax today."

"Sort of. You were right about the energy feeling off. Especially right now. There's a strong sense of danger. An evil."

"Really? I have been feeling really weird. But I am, you know, of a certain age. Time of change. Et cetera."

Sal lightly places a hand on Paula's wrist. "Oh wait—it's coming off you. Definitely. A bad energy."

"What?"

"I'm sorry, I have to call it like I feel it. In the air around you. On your wrist. You're bubbling with it."

Paula steps back.

"I don't fuck around with this stuff," Sal continues. "I just know what I'm talking about. I'm sorry, I can't be around this. It's much too intense. I have to get out of here. I always do the steam pool before bed to cleanse the bad energy. Get myself roasting like a ham and then I pass out like a light. Take care." She gets up and pats Paula on the arm, then walks away.

Paula touches her own wrist. Does it feel evil? Bad? She can't tell. Her gaze drifts out the window at the lake, the children running along the beach, then back inside at the bar patrons enjoying each other's company, laughing, sharing oysters and truffle fries. At the bar, there is Joanie, sitting on the same barstool as before.

Paula walks over to join her. "No Donut Blast for you?"

"I don't use a cellphone. I'm old-fashioned."

"Smart, honestly."

"Your friends aren't with you? I thought I saw you together earlier."

"Oh, Mikey had to put her kids to bed, and Lisa went to check on her husband. We're meeting up again later. I wasn't being very accommodating."

"Are you sure about that?"

"Yeah, I was being weird. Really weird."

"Weird is good. Weird is everything. The weirder, the better. If you're not going wild, you're not going anywhere! That's what I've always said. And look at me. Living my life to the fullest. I've learned some lessons in my time, let me tell you, love. Seems your friends aren't as interested in spending time with you as you thought. I saw you running away from them."

"I kind of did. It was sort of funny. I got some twenty-year-old dude to haul me up out of the pool."

"Your life is more fun than you're letting on."

"It's really not at all."

The bartender places a Too Much Blush in front of Paula.

"I got you a double," Joanie says.

Paula takes a sip and instantly feels elated. She slams the rest of it in one gulp, ignoring the small voice in her head that reminds her she isn't supposed to get drunk again.

"Another?" Joanie asks.

Paula nods at the bartender, and soon another slushy pink drink is placed in front of her. Joanie grabs her wrists and holds them out between the two of them.

"I feel so connected to you! You really remind me of myself. You've got a fire in you that you don't want to let out. But you should. You need to. It's insulting to keep it in, to keep it to yourself. It's only growing more toxic as you let it build up inside. That's going to hurt you more than letting it out would hurt anyone else. You just need to be honest. How often do you lie to yourself? For these so-called friends?"

Paula feels the fire that Joanie has described, sharp and warm and inviting. The heat coursing through her body is comforting and exhilarating.

"I guess I do want to tell people what I want from them, even though they'll probably say no. I'm tired of expecting things from them. I'm just not good at telling people what I want."

"Some people need a little push. A shove. A shock. That's why behaving out of character can be so powerful. You need to rattle them so hard that they have to give you what you want. And if they don't, you have to take it from them."

Paula says yes to everything, goes to swim meets and anniversary parties, picks things up for her friends that they don't want to travel into the city to get. Then she drives all the way to the suburbs to deliver them.

"I really freaked them out. I screamed, I shouted, I said the meanest things to them. I haven't been acting like myself at all. "

"No, you've been acting like me." Joanie's eyes widen, again so intense that Paula can't look away. She feels the fire burning in her toes, her wrists, her thighs, her chest. And then she notices tiny flames circling Joanie's pupils. She jumps off her barstool, knocking over a plastic bowl of nuts. Joanie laughs.

A group of people coming in from the pools, dressed in jeans and fun tops, sweatshirts and yoga pants, pass through the bar. None of them pays the slightest attention to the fiery-eyed woman laughing maniacally with her Pepto-Bismol–toned beverage. But they do look pitifully at Paula, who's crouched on the floor, bun askew, gathering up dusty floor nuts.

"I'm helping you, dummy!" Joanie says. "You couldn't take control of your own life, so I took over for you!"

Paula stops gathering the nuts to gape at Joanie. A lick of periwinkle fire escapes her mouth.

Paula jumps up and bumps into a high-top, sending two empty martini glasses crashing to the ground. "Are you fucking kidding me?" She pushes a stool between herself and Joanie.

"Mom, that person's being crazy again!" The kid with the scooter zips past, followed as ever by his mother.

"Shh, we don't call people crazy, okay?"

Paula knows they mean her, not Joanie. Her face is heating up again as Joanie's fury makes her blood roil. She flings the bowl of nuts at Joanie and runs outside, away from her.

She rushes along the walkways, past the "NO RUNNING" signs, past the tipsy people deciding whether they're going to hook up after their long day of convention meetings, past parents letting their children stay up past bedtime. She's left her phone in the bar, can't call or text Lisa and Mikey. Then she sees them. Just the two of them, no children or spouses. Just like they planned. Right on time.

She runs up to them, panting. "Okay, so, I think I was possessed when I was freaking out at you guys."

"You must have been, because it's so not like you."

"Possessed by what?" Lisa asks.

"I think a ghost, or a demon. A hybrid, maybe. I'm not an expert on these things."

"I think demons possess and ghosts haunt."

"Is this for like a murder mystery game? Because I told you, I hate those fucking things," Mikey says, sipping her drink.

Paula starts to cry. She doesn't know how to explain herself or what to do. She can feel her body heat still rising, her chest knotting, but she has no clue how to stave off another possession. Mikey and Lisa look at each other and then lean over to hug her, one on each side.

"I know this sounds wild, but I'm pretty sure that's why I yelled at you." Paula wipes her snotty face on her once-pristine caftan.

"This is a bit weird. Like, are you making this up to avoid taking accountability for your actions?"

"Mikey, I don't think Paula would make this up."

"It's a lot easier to believe than possession. Come on!"

"I am telling you, I keep getting this feeling like my entire body is on fire and I want to attack everyone and be monstrous!"

"Could it be perimenopause?" Lisa asks.

"Yes, but not in this instance! Please. A glamorous dead woman is possessing me!"

Mikey takes Paula's hand to calm her down. "Hmm. I'm not religious—I mean, I believe in astrology, but is that going to help here? Do we need to get a priest or something?"

"I was baptized," Lisa offers, stroking Paula's hair.

"That's something. Pass me my drink so I can think!"

Lisa hands over Mikey's drink. Out of the corner of her eye, Paula sees the edge of Joanie's caftan flare as she slinks around the corner. It reminds her that she has nothing to apologize for. Joanie was right. She just said was what needed to be said. Her head drops to her chest as the searing sensation rushes over her skin and through her veins again. She wants to lash out, to smash a wine bottle and go at her friends with the sharp glass.

"Holy water? That's also something. Ha, remember when we saw all of the *Exorcist* movies and *Repossessed* all in one weekend?"

"That was such a great marathon! Linda Blair really deserved a better career."

They're off on a tangent, as usual. Paula doesn't mean anything to them.

"I don't mean anything to you!"

"Of course you do, don't be a jackass!" Mikey says.

"If I had a husband, you'd probably be off having a threesome with him right now. If either of you comes close to my husband, even thinks of laying your filthy pussy on him, I will make your life a living hell!"

"Whoa, Paula, is this the possession? You don't even like men."

"Your children come over to my tiny apartment to draw on the walls with permanent marker. And Dave is a terrible conversationalist and probably terrible in bed. No wonder you want to sleep with my husband!" She stands bolt upright, startling Lisa and Mikey, and points at each of them, wagging her finger like a schoolmarm. "You think I'm joking? Because you think my life is a fucking joke? You bitches, living your normal-ass lives! I CAN DO WHATEVER I WANT AND I CAN DESTROY YOU!"

Paula lunges at Mikey, her hands balled into fists, ready to pummel. Mikey leaps away, past another "NO RUNNING" sign.

"What the fun, P? Why are you being so aggressive? I didn't do anything!"

"YOU NEVER DO! NOT FOR ME!"

"Ah, shit. You *are* possessed. Goddamnit," Lisa says.

Paula races after Mikey in pursuit. An elderly man in the lap pool, seeing the commotion, dunks himself under the water.

"Paula, time for tough love, okay? You gotta get over whatever this is. I will buy you a pina colada and a whole pizza! I know you love a whole pizza!" Mikey screams.

"I ALREADY ATE A WHOLE PIZZA BY MYSELF! BY MYSELF! Because the two of you were fucking around with people who are not more important than me. I WILL GET MY REVENGE ON YOU AND YOUR WHOLE FAMILIES!"

Mikey stops to rest, leaning on the back of a lounge chair, breathing heavily. Lisa catches up and puts an arm around her. "Stop this, Paula."

Paula jumps onto the lounge chair. "Stop this, Paula!" she says mockingly, watching a little silver flame flicker out of her nostril. "Shut up, you little weakling! The two of you had the nerve to bring your husband and children here even though you knew I wanted to see you alone. I could tear the limbs off them all with my bare hands! And I will. I'll rip their arms from their torsos, I'll shove those arms into their mouths and suffocate them. And then pop their heads off like the tops of those disgusting low-calorie beers Dave loves so much. I'll sidle up to the family grill and fry their heads until the meat falls off the bone and then I'll make the two of you handbags out of the skulls!" Paula cackles, tossing her head back.

Mikey's crying now. Tears stream down her face. "You know I hate body horror, Paula."

"You couldn't even pick me up from the fucking hospital when I thought I had cancer! BECAUSE OF ONE STUPID BRIDGE! THERE ARE OTHER ROUTES! LONGER ROUTES! TAKE THE LONG WAY! I'M WORTH IT!"

Everyone in the lap pool is cowering in the far corner. An employee holds a pool net over his head like a weapon.

"Paula, I am so sorry about that. I don't think we deserve to die over it. But yeah, that wasn't cool!" Lisa says.

"We did fuck that up. I'm sorry. We're both sorry, Paula."

"There is no Paula! She is DEAD and soon you can join her!"

"Why don't you grow up, you shitty little demon!" Lisa shouts, pushing Paula with both hands. She stumbles off the chair and falls backward into the pool, where she thrashes in the water. Her mind flashes to the fear on her friends' faces, the bros hiding in the corner, the tension in her limbs, in her neck, in each finger. Then she allows herself to sink to the bottom, her poly-cotton blend billowing around her like peony petals. Her mind goes blank.

When she breaks the surface and opens her eyes, her pulse has slowed to normal, and her skin is cool, though her mouth feels scalded, like every word that came out of it has left little burns on her tongue. She plunges back into the water, shakes herself clear of all the rage and worry and panic.

She shoots up again. "Okay, I'm fine! I'm fine!"

"You're okay?" Lisa says.

"Yeah, I am."

"Can we really trust you?" Mikey asks.

"Let's see."

Paula gets out of the water and dries herself off, drops the towel on the pool deck. Her friends watch her pace back and forth. After a few minutes, she feels heat rising from her feet into her chest and head.

"Well?" Mikey says.

Paula walks over to Mikey and growls in her face, then raises her head to the sky and lets a lick of flame escape her lips.

"So, not okay," Lisa says.

Paula stalks toward them, her fingers outstretched like claws. As she lunges, they move aside so that she crashes into the pool. Gradually, again, she feels a sense of calm returning, a light tingling along her skin as she floats to the surface. On her back, she looks up at the stars, so beautiful and so clear here, far from the city. She looks at her friends and smiles.

Mikey and Lisa jump into the pool with her, and the three of them hug, sopping wet.

"I'm sorry I scared you and threatened you and called you bitches. I don't really want to murder you!"

"Paula, we love you," Lisa says.

"We love you, you're so important to us."

"You're allowed to say things to us, things we might not want to hear."

"Of course you are," Mikey agrees. "One time you told me you hated my chunky highlights, and at the time I thought I'd never forgive you, but I did."

"Mikey!"

"But for real, you might be right about some of that stuff," Mikey continues. "Like, maybe the bitch thing is true. For sure! But also some of that other stuff. I know I can get lost in my own shit sometimes."

"I definitely know I can. You are *our* Paula. You have to know that. You can't get rid of us."

They smother her with hugs, sobbing into her body. The three of them huddle together, clutching at each other.

Paula starts to shake. She steps back from her friends fearfully, moves all the way to the side of the pool, and grips the edge. Her body vibrates, her head shoots straight up, and a long, thin flame escapes her mouth, dissipating into smoke. She just notices that she's cracked the concrete with her hands before she begins hacking like a cat coughing up a hairball. She turns to face the pool deck just before pink frothy barf floods out of her mouth. There's a brief pause, then more and more of it comes. After one final heave, she horks a pink loogie onto the pool deck.

"Am I okay now? I feel okay."

"I have kids, and that was the most disgusting thing I've ever seen," Mikey says.

"All right, out! Outta there!" the hotel employee shouts. "No pushing and no jumping. And shit, what is that? No whatever that is." He points at the puke with the pool net. "You're out. Banned!"

Paula starts to laugh, but Mikey and Lisa are dismayed.

"But we got so organized to be here!" Lisa says.

"I don't want to hear it! You're worse than those guys over there."

"She's possessed by a demon!" Mikey insists.

"Like I haven't heard that one before!" The scooter boy whizzes by, squirting his water gun in all directions, hitting several guests and the employee. "Aw shit, now this kid again."

The employee shuffles off after the kid, and the other guests in the pool area gradually resume their activities, muttering to each other. No one pays the three women any attention as they exit the pool.

"That guy will never remember us if we go in the crowded adults-only pool," Paula whispers.

"You think?"

Mikey finishes her drink and drapes herself in towels. "Look, I'm hidden! No one can see me!"

"Let's do it. They're all drunk or horny in there. They'll probably love us for causing trouble!" Paula says.

"Yeah, fuck that shit. We've been through a lot," Lisa says.

Stashing their belongings under a plastic chair on the pool deck, they climb into the adults-only pool. *Finally, we can relax*, Paula thinks. She points out the Fucking King, who is miming jerking off on the back of a woman's head while his friends high-five beside him. "That little shit has been such a nightmare since I got here. How do I channel a demon into him?"

"I'd love to make that guy uncomfortable for even one minute."

"His frontal lobe might not yet be capable of feeling shame."

The three of them lean into each other and cackle. Surrounded by the warmth of the water and her friends, Paula feels whole again.

"I'll go get us more drinks," she says. "We didn't even get to cheers my baptism!"

"Are you sure?"

"Yeah, you just threw up the most anyone has ever thrown up."

"I feel great. That was a hard reset. And look, there's no line for the bar."

She climbs the pool steps. Her eyes rise to focus on her hotel room window. There is Joanie, caftan flowing around her, staring down. Paula smiles, and Joanie smiles back.

The sky is starting to get peachy and light. She sees a construction site, this one excavated, with another big sign in front. Opening her backpack, she examines the stencil—it's too damaged to use again. A neatly folded receipt for the spray paint jumps out from the inside pocket. She bends over to snatch it, but a gust of wind picks it up and deposits it into the deep foundation pit at the construction site. Concrete will cover it, no one will ever notice it in the sub-basement of a glistening new condo tower. She even paid cash. No paper trail, except for an actual slip of paper printed with "$16.94" soaked in rain. She grabs her stencil and tears it into pieces, tosses them into the hole too. She can always make another one. Without the stencil, she could still destroy the sign, but she wants to stay on message.

HERE I GO AGAIN

The yoga pants are tight. Kirstie's going to wear them out of the store and straight to a class. A new phase of life deserves a new pair of MindfulLegs pants, her clothing staple. Despite how thin her legs are, these pants look painted on, like the 1990s *Vanity Fair* cover of Demi Moore she has pinned on an inspiration mood board in her office. The smallest size is actually a little too small for her. Though she normally loves to barge out of the fitting room to examine the clothing in better light and the company of others, she doesn't this time. She yanks off the skin-tight XXS, puts on the XS, and takes a few breaths to compose herself. Then she contemplates her body, mouths hello to her reflection, waves, and thinks, *This is the best version of myself.* She looks just how she imagines she always looks, was always meant to look. Honey-blond curls, perfectly maintained bangs, a banging bod, skin as pale as a pristine dinner plate, and abs rippling like beach sand at low tide.

When she finally emerges, she leaves the XXS balled in the corner of the fitting room. The yoga pants she came in wearing are draped neatly over her narrow forearm.

"Could I keep these on and buy them?" she asks the clerk at the cash desk. "I've got the tag right here. And can I donate these pants to the Yoga Pants for the Poor program?"

"Um, yes, that's not what it's called ... as long as they're lightly used, sure."

"Oh, well then you might not accept them. I've used them pretty harshly. These pants have been subjected to sweat, intense stretching, and some very serious poses."

"I'm sure they're fine."

The clerk smiles, takes the pants from her, and deposits them in a hamper filled with other worn yoga pants.

Kirstie hands over the tag, and the clerk rings in her purchase.

"How would you like to pay?"

"I'm so happy to contribute to a program for people who don't have the privileges I do. That is what feminism looks like."

"What method of payment would you like to use?"

"Oh, credit please." Kirstie taps her thick black card over the pay pad. "We all need to be doing more. The world has really changed, and with all the white supremacy, those of us with more can't sit idly by. I know you get this. You work for a company that cares about health and wellness. Which is so important. So many people have to do so much just to get by."

"Printed or emailed receipt?"

"Email, please. Thank you for your help today."

"You're welcome."

She reaches expectantly for a bag, then remembers she's wearing her purchase. "Just one more thing. Can I ask you a question?" The clerk says nothing. "Did you change the sizing on these pants? Not you personally, but the company. There's something a smidge different about these compared to all the ones I've purchased before? Just out of curiosity. I do love these, though. I mean, I love yoga. Of course. Obviously. What's not to love?"

@KirstieKares
Just had the most amazing conversation with a customer service worker about giving back to the community. Those of us who can afford to buy $200 yoga pants need to be aware of those who don't have any yoga pants at all. #GiveBack #YogaForEveryone #CheckYourPrivilege

In a city where no one can ever be too rich or too thin, Kirstie is living her best life. #ILoveYoga. She crosses the street to the closest Y R U Not Doing Yoga? studio, swipes her YVIP card, and slides up the escalator to the prime studio on the eighteenth floor. It's noon, and it's crammed with lunch-hour try-hards. She's not used to so many people in her preferred studio, but she made a choice today to buy new pants and donate her used ones, and later she has important plans she's committed to, so this is the only option, since she can't miss her daily yoga time. #TheOnlyTimeToDoSomethingGreatIsNow. A bit long, but she'll work on it. If she were going to get a tattoo, that might be it.

She swoops her curls into a bun on top of her head and strokes the fabric of her new pants, her fingertips proudly running along her strong thigh muscles underneath. The only space in the room is near the front, a tight spot between two people engaged in conversation about the best place in town to get a poke bowl. Nattering on about sauces and extras.

"I know the oceans are depleting, but I just love tuna, baby!"

"Excuse me." Kirstie nudges between them and unfurls her mat.

“Sorry, I guess. Anyway, we should definitely check out the place on Hornby. The woman who runs the place is so sweet. And they have Dole Whip.”

“Holy shit, Dole Whip! Want.”

“Excuse me, I just can’t think about food before yoga. It’s a very distracting headspace for me,” Kirstie says.

“Sorry? We’re just chatting.”

She looks from one person to the other, bows her head, and puts her hands together like a prayer sent up to stop all annoying conversations. The women start whispering, but then their instructor takes to the front of the room.

Kirstie is supposed to be letting go, focusing on the poses and nothing else, moving through each one with purpose. But the woman in front of her has a strange, distracting way of breathing. A rustle through her nose, as if the mucus in her nostrils were tree branches brimming with leaves and each breath a strong breeze. But Kirstie can do this. Yoga is her happy place. And this evening, she’s getting her groove back. After years away from it, she’s ready to attend her first activist meeting. So she’s made this sacrifice: lunchtime yoga.

As her body moves, her brain runs through different scenarios for how the evening will play out, how the meeting will go, and who might be there. She saw the event shared on social media by someone in an elite women-only yoga group on Framebook: Jessie from university (newly single, going on bike-and-brew tours). Kirstie was curious to see what Jessie was up to, as well as very empathetic to her heartbreak, and saw that she’d commented on the event page that she was sad not to be attending.

Feminists for Change: Call for New Members

Thursday Night

7 p.m.

NoTERFs No SWERFs

418 East 3rd Avenue
main level, use the door along the alley side

Kirstie didn't even click to read the full description of the organization. All she needed to know was that they were planning action and needed volunteers. She selected "Attending," saved the address and date in her calendar, and set a reminder notification for herself. In total, fifty people have RSVP'd as attending, another eighty as maybes. According to social media event attendance math, that means there'll likely be around thirty people. A large number, but not unreasonable for learning and retaining their names for the next meeting. She'll bring her iPad and use her Framebook app to keep track of them so she doesn't look like a jerk the next time she sees everyone.

Somehow, the class is over. She's been distracted the whole time. She catches herself in the full-length wall mirror, standing with her head stretched down between her spread legs, everyone around her slowly packing up to head back to their respective offices. Without changing position, she mouths hello to herself, tells herself that she will do better next time. She lost herself in the wrong way today, but it was the first lunchtime class in a long time, and she's not used to it, the new people. New people are an opportunity, but also new people can be difficult. She waits until everyone has left the studio before going to the YVIP locker room, where people shower in the deep stalls, hot water blasting so that steam settles over the mirrors.

As an undergrad, Kirstie had been involved. A member of groups, clubs, organizations. Safe Campus Initiative, Feminists for Health & Wellness, the Protest Signmakers Collective, Rich Bitches for Change. Her bedroom had started out decorated with boy band posters which, over time, were covered up with activist slogans, protest signs, and two huge inspiration boards with collages of her activist heroes.

She was always there to take control of a committee, to make a protest plan, to make sure everyone had their signs ready to go before they hit the pavement. She would fact-check and spell-check. Even when others weren't in agreement with her leadership or questioned her decisions or spoke candidly while she was trying to delegate.

But after she got into grad school, she found herself getting offers that paid. A professor gave her a nudge to a job that suited her. Her skills paid off in the corporate world. Financial planning required organization and navigating volatile personalities too. And in many ways, it was a relief. No yelling about who was in charge or why anyone was in charge, no fighting over a collective idea. She could be in control.

It's been ten years now. She spends most of her time at work with men at least ten to fifteen years older than her. They seem to respect her but don't ask much of her; certainly she's not invited to their networking events or golf games. On weekends, she hikes in the morning and does yoga in the evening, when she doesn't have a friend's birthday dinner or tickets to a show. And sometimes even when she does. The spark of enjoying life is there, but not the something more she always assumed would also be present. So now she is trying to snatch back joy with her mid-length French-manicured nails.

The area is dark without street lights, and Kirstie's never spent much time in this corner of the city. Kitsilano isn't far away in terms of distance, but she hasn't ever had the need to pop into this once industrial zone that's been taken over by breweries and tech start-ups and condos. She is not a beer drinker, which always felt like an issue when she was in university, but now drinking cocktails and wine doesn't make her look like a social failure.

Since it's not well lit, the building addresses are almost invisible. She drives around the block again, certain she's in the right place, before parking next to a scraggy shrub near the alley. Down the lane, she can see light escaping a propped-open door.

Her custom leather work tote is filled with meeting supplies: binder, folders, two notebooks, and a selection of pens and highlighters, as well as her iPad and Apple Pencil stowed in a silk slipcover in the large pocket. She has her old feminist classics in her bag, still cluttered with tabs and flags. Her favourite trench coat gives the right vibe for navigating a new space, and she feels a lightness as she clicks through the dark in her low heels, swinging her bag at her side. Her Apple Watch beeps a notification. She's ten minutes early, which to Kirstie is just on time.

A kid who looks no older than eighteen walks past her into the brightly lit room.

"Nice shoes."

"Oh, thank you. Hello."

She's not the only one who's early. Standing in the open doorway, she sees there aren't many free chairs, most of them being occupied by young people in jeans and crewnecks and tiny toques. Denim and leather jackets are slung over the backs of the metal folding chairs. Backpacks and tote bags dot the concrete floor. She seems to be the only person with an expensive leather bag. The person she assumed was a kid takes the centre of the floor, welcomes everyone, and says something about a land acknowledgment while Kirstie moves toward an empty chair at the end of a row. Everyone turns to look at her as her heels clack on the parquet floor.

"Sorry, sorry! Just getting my bearings here."

Several people mutter "shh." She sits down and rests her bag on her lap, doesn't take off her jacket.

"I'm Han, they/them. First, I'm so happy you're here, and I want to thank everyone for leaving your home on a dark, cold night for this. And to all of those who have come together before tonight to help with organizing, I wouldn't feel confident and comfortable without you here. We are nothing without community, and you are all so important to what we're doing. Our goal is to do something impactful that will disrupt. And we think this next action will be able to do that. So, we need to work on logistics to make sure we have a solid core and aren't leaving anything too loose or unfinished."

Han crosses the floor and asks if anyone has anything they want to say, any questions, any concerns, any contributions. Listening, Kirstie tries to take notes about it all. They're planning action for a few weeks from now. Once the floor is open, she loses track of what exactly is happening. Information is filtering in from many different voices. She jumps on her iPad and starts trying to find everyone on ZChirp as they speak so she can follow them.

"I'm Ang, she/her. I'm going to be managing and organizing volunteers. So if anyone has questions about that, see me after the meeting is adjourned."

"Mila, she/her. I'm concerned about safety. We need to make sure that we're prioritizing the safety of those who are most likely to be arrested. Straight white cis women have to step in. I'd love to have volunteers who are ready to be on that front line."

Kirstie's watch pings. A reminder to take her supplements. Everyone looks around. She silences it, sees that no one else is talking, and stands up.

"What kind of supplies do we need? I can cater the next event, if that helps," she says.

Small coughs and throat clearing around the room.

"Okay, noted. Any further questions, please talk to those who are organizing those particular areas," Han says.

Kirstie remains standing and raises her hand.

"I also have so many ideas myself. When I used to be involved in activism I really put myself on the line, you know. Hashtag No Fear! And I think my experience could really benefit a group of this size.

I have also taken three different corporate training seminars on conflict resolution."

The room is silent.

"Okay, let's finish up for now," Han says. "If you have action items, I'll be in touch about those. Spreadsheets will be sent out to those who need them, and any information to volunteers will be sent out by those who have the relevant details. It's wonderful to see so many new faces here. Don't forget to share your information with us before you leave. Thank you, and I appreciate all you folks coming out tonight. It's very heartening to see so many of you here."

Everyone gets up, folds their own chairs, and returns them to stacks at the edge of the room. Someone in a boiler suit hauls a table out the back door. People splinter into small groups to talk or wave and say goodbye before heading out into the night. Everyone seems to know each other, and the ones who don't are being introduced by their friends.

Kirstie knows she has a lot to offer. She has lots of experience and has the time and money to provide whatever they need. She spots Ang talking to a group, including Han. Ang is taller than everyone there and seems to have a calm way about her, despite the intense energy in the room. Possibly she also practises yoga.

Kirstie gets up from her chair, slides her stationery into her leather bag, grabs her chair under one arm, and walks over to the group.

"Hello, I'm Kirstie. Great to be here. Great to meet you. What great energy!" She reaches out her hand for someone to shake, but no one takes it.

"Hi, just a moment," Han says. "If you wait right there, we can speak to you in a minute. Sorry, we don't usually interrupt when people are in conversation."

"Of course, yes. I am listening and learning!" Kirstie steps to the side and opens her phone, checks to see if she has any new followers. Not yet. She's still at 1,755. After a few scrolls through her the yoga influencer accounts she follows, Han and Ang turn to her.

"Sorry I interrupted. I just got very excited. Han, very inspiring words today. You're just really articulate, and so young! I'm impressed."

"Okay. You should know it's problematic to tell people they're articulate or comment on their age. But I am very impressive. I appreciate your enthusiasm. We do need a lot of energy," Han says.

"Han, I know you're busy and probably tired," Ang says. "Why don't you head out? I'll talk to our energetic newbie."

Han smiles, waves, and leaves through the door into the alley. Everyone else follows their lead except for Ang, who watches the room emptying out. "I'm the one with the keys," she says, jingling them against her clipboard.

"Again, I'm Kirstie, KirstieKares on ZChirp. Thanks again. I'm ready to do whatever I need to."

"First time?"

"Well no, I used to be very active, but I took a break, built a career. But it's just not satisfying, you know?"

"Hm. Did you sign up? Leave contact information?"

"Oh no, I'll do that right away." Ang hands her the clipboard. With the pen that's attached by a string, Kirstie fills in all her information. "Anyway, as I said, money, resources, hard labour, I'm here for it all!"

"Thanks. We appreciate enthusiasm. And we'll be in touch."

Kirstie waves and heads out. Before she starts her car, she checks her phone. Several notifications. She now has a few new followers on ZChirp and a DM from someone named BadAng.

> **@BadAng** Thanks so much for coming tonight. We're already in the planning stage and things are moving quickly, but we appreciate the support. Please don't be discouraged by the intensity. Stick it out.

@KirstieKares Thank you so much! I have so many ideas to share. I'm not discouraged. I love to lead on the front lines. I know I'll become a huge asset to the organization!

@BadAng Ha ha! We aren't really an organization but a collective. Thank you, though. We do need enthusiasm.

That was a fast reply, and a good sign. She speeds home, charged by the prospect of change.

"It's so thrilling to be involved again."

Kirstie stands behind the fresh juice station at her kitchen island. Prosecco, sparkling water, and four litres of organic kombucha serve as mixers for those who want to spice up their brunch beverages.

"Have you read Deidre Wind? Watched her thirty-part series? It's on the premium subscription. Do you like her?" Lila asks, holding out her glass for a top-up.

"Like her? I'm obsessed with her. I love strong Black women," Kirstie says.

"That's great. But she's white."

"Oh, I don't know what I was thinking. Maybe because that Black influencer loves her."

"True. But that influencer definitely does love white women. Look at her book club selections."

"Yeah, my brain is just all over the place these days. Thinking about work and activism, and I don't have time for thirty-part streaming anythings," Kirstie says.

"Yeah, I really don't know. She's not for everyone. I'm not even sure I subscribe to all of that anyway, but interesting to think about."

Kirstie empties the dregs of the prosecco bottle into her glass, takes a gulp, and walks back to the wine fridge to get more bottles.

"I would love for us to start our own group, maybe. We can do it just like this, but you know, plan for the future. Find a cause to take on."

"I already volunteer with seniors downtown three days a week, and I'm on two non-profit boards," Coral says, breaking off a piece of a gluten-free croissant.

"Hey! I'm on three boards. Hashtag Board Life!" Lila says, holding out her glass for a cheers.

From a new bottle, Kirstie refills her own glass and holds it up, but they've moved on to talking about the latest dead-girl, gritty limited series on premium cable. She can never seem to get into these shows, doesn't understand why beautiful people would want to make themselves look like ugly, regular people.

She brings out the next round of fruits and pastries, but Lila and Coral both have to take their children to improv class. So Kirstie sends them home with doggy bags for their kids and puts all the leftovers in the garbage disposal and their glasses and dishes in the dishwasher. The house basically cleans itself.

She takes another swig of her drink. It's not even noon and she's already preparing for a tipsy afternoon nap.

@KirstieKares

Replying to **@BadAng**

I love having people over to talk about what we can do to change the world and feeding them healthy snacks while we do it. Dietary restrictions and allergies are real. We got angry about sexual predators, but we also talked about how yoga practice and hair brushing are acts of defiance. #AngryFeministsForChange #PrettyHairDontCare

@KirstieKares

Replying to @**__HAN__**

Love to know there is a badass like Han out there crushing it and making things happen behind the scenes. #FeministsForChange

@__HAN_

Replying to **@KirstieKares**

Not sure what you're talking about, but I appreciate the support.

Han doesn't remember her. There were too many people at the meeting, that's all. Before she can remind Han that they already met, the mimosas take hold, and she's down for an afternoon nap.

On the last day of Kirstie's undergrad, there was supposed to be a protest outside the political science student centre office. A grad student had been accused of assault, yet no one seemed to care. The investigation was closed and there he was, TA-ing his class as if nothing had happened.

Kirstie's group had been planning the protest for weeks. But then, days before it was supposed to happen, there was radio silence. Not a word from anyone in the group. She tried to contact people, but got no response. She could only assume it was cancelled.

A week later, the protest was written up in the university newspaper. Photos of the group confronting the department head. Signs. Their determined faces. And she was nowhere to be seen.

Kirstie comes to the next meeting more prepared. Simple clothes. No notebooks. A Tory Burch canvas tote instead of a leather handbag. Her oldest pair of leather Adidas, jeans, and a blue crewneck. The group has grown. Everyone's still at least ten years younger than she is. But they haven't commented on that. They haven't commented much on anything she's said or chirped. In her folding chair at the back of the room, she does a breathing exercise, imagining a room full of mirrors, herself reflected in her XS yoga pants. She is centred, she is herself, she is here, she is enough.

She's brought out of it by Han's voice as they take the floor and invite Ang up to speak.

"Your time is important, and we want to maximize that. This is our last time getting together before next week's action, and barring any last-minute changes, it should all go according to the plans I'll lay out today. I'll be asking you to take on particular roles in your groups."

"Thanks, Ang. Coordination is key. We have to listen to each other and do everything with respect."

Kirstie puts her hand up. No one says anything. She stretches it up a little higher. "Excuse me. I just wanted to say something."

"Okay, this is an open forum," Han says.

Kirstie stands up. "I am just so grateful to be here. Hashtag Blessed, and I want everyone to know that I'm a real team player and just love what you're doing, and I do have some experience from my earlier days and hope you won't judge me for being in my late thirties. Just kidding! I think! Anyway, I wanted to donate some money, and no one has been able to tell me where to do that. So. I know orgs always need money, and being privileged means I'm obligated to provide funding. Coupled with my experience as a leader at work and in activist circles, it just all comes together. Can't wait to do more! If anyone has questions for me I'll be right here!"

"Okay, I'll get someone to connect with you about that. Now, Ang is going to come around and talk to everyone. So please gather in your groups, and we'll be one more big step on our way toward this action. Thanks so much!"

Kirstie stands around, waiting to be assigned to a group, but it looks like everyone already has their groups. She excuses herself to no one and goes to find the bathroom, wandering the narrow hallways, opening every door to find empty rooms and closets. There's an old staircase at the end of the hall. She looks down it. It's dark.

"Hello?" she calls.

"You looking for the bathroom?"

"Shit! You startled me, Han."

"I didn't know you swore."

"I've sworn lots of times in my life."

"Teasing. The bathroom is down there. The light is broken, but we have a flashlight." Han reaches down into the dark stairwell and pulls out a small silver flashlight, hands it to Kirstie.

"Thanks."

"Not a problem."

"Listen, I'm not here to cause trouble. I'm here to help."

"I didn't say you were."

"Well, the way you spoke to me was not very ..."

"Not very what?"

"Nothing. I really need to use the restroom."

Kirstie turns on the flashlight and makes her way downstairs. The bathroom is a large room with one toilet and two sinks and rusted old pipes. Luckily, there's a working light in there. There's no hook for her bag, so she clutches it to her chest while she pees. The toilet won't flush. She jiggles the handle. Nothing. She screams and punches the industrial toilet paper dispenser. It pops opens, and a large roll of paper jumps out and rolls across the floor. Someone knocks at the door.

"Someone's in here!" Kirstie shouts.

"Okay. Thought I heard a scream. Thought there might be a rat."

She starts to do her breathing again. Imagines herself, her perfect self, then releases an exhale. She manifests no rats, a rat-free environment. The power of the law of attraction, but in reverse. The law of repulsion.

"Sorry, can't get the toilet to flush," she shouts.

"Just gotta hold the handle down for like thirty seconds."

She holds down the handle until the toilet flushes, then fetches the roll of paper from the other end of the room. It fell on its side, and the bottom edges of the paper are dripping wet. She tries to put it back in the dispenser but can't figure it out. She leaves it on top, still wet. What can she do?

The mirror is dirty and rusted, but she's thankful to see a part of her face reflected back. She breathes. She scrubs her hands. She tucks some hairs that escaped during the toilet drama back into her bun.

Han is sitting in the dark on the stairs outside the bathroom, looking at their phone. "Where's the flashlight?"

"Oh, I left it inside. I'll go get it. Also, I can't get the toilet paper dispenser to stay closed. I almost lost a whole roll. Ha ha ha. I'm so sorry!" Kirstie rushes back into the bathroom.

"Did you try?" Han asks from the doorway.

"Try what?"

"To fix the toilet paper dispenser?"

Kirstie hands over the flashlight. "I tried, but I've never done anything like that before. I'm not very handy."

Han sighs and goes to a small wooden cabinet in the hallway, pulls out a tool box. "I thought you said you were ready to do anything for the cause."

"I didn't mean to break anything. It was an accident."

"I can fix it. Fixing things is what I do."

"I don't know what to say. I'm here to help, and I didn't mean to do what I did. It just happened. I'm not doing anything wrong here. And your attitude isn't helping me feel like I can be helpful."

"Some people make mistakes and don't apologize, and some people try to fix things and make them better. I'm not saying there are only two kinds of people, but I'm just saying."

Han holds the flashlight in their mouth as they riffle through the tool box, pulling out screwdrivers and wrenches and loose nails.

"It sounds like you think I'm a person who makes messes and breaks things on purpose."

Han slams a wrench back down into the box, and the flashlight drops out of their mouth. "Don't you ever just think of yourself as an asshole who makes mistakes, like a normal person?"

"No. I'm a good person who's trying. And I try my hardest not to make any mistakes, because being good is really important to me."

"Sometimes when I'm trying to take a shit, I have to give up because it's not ready to come out. Something to consider."

Han takes the flashlight and tools into the bathroom, leaving Kirstie in the dark.

At home, she takes in what Han said. She draws a bath, uses her auras to determine which essential oils are best to add, and leaves her phone in the living room to charge while she soaks. She turns on her bathroom flat-screen. It's the news. She hardly ever looks at the news—too painful. With the remote she mutes the television and watches silent footage of bombs dropping, children screaming, a crocodile swallowing a whole goat, and a celebrity pushing a stroller with three newly adopted babies from three different countries. It makes her cry so much she has to put on extra serum.

When she's dried off and in her pyjamas, she sits at the kitchen island with a glass of low-calorie cider and dips baby cucumbers into celery juice. While she crunches, she checks her phone. No new messages. She needs to chirp with purpose. To think about what Han said, what the meetings mean to her. The group's hashtag alone is inspiring. She fires off a few chirps.

@KirstieKares
Learning and growth take time, but never stop trying. Always strive for more. There are so many who do not have the advantages you have. Think before you talk and act! #FeministsForChange #CheckYourPrivilege

@KirstieKares
Had some real revelations over the past few days. Really trying to stay on my growth and healing. #FeministsForChange

@KirstieKares
Spent a good hour with other incredible women making our bodies ready to take on the world #YogaForAll #StretchAndBitch #FeministsForChange

She's taken to chirping only every two hours so she isn't constantly online, but when she does, she has a few at the ready. And it's hard not to constantly share in the lead up to the protest. Well, she's not supposed to call it a protest. An action. And she's not supposed to tell people about it yet, but she's bursting.

@KirstieKares
I can barely contain my excitement for the work we are doing, wink wink! #FeministsForChange

Once she gets in bed, like a kid before Christmas, her legs are full of energy, constantly twitching. She sets her phone on the nightstand and turns out the light, closes her eyes, and thinks about the ocean, vast and beautiful. Says "om" quietly, but loud enough that she can feel her mouth and nostrils vibrate.

An hour later, she still can't sleep. She gets her phone and opens the app. Slips on her glasses. Replies to her earlier chirps, some rechirps.

There's a direct message from Han, who's gone private and locked their account.

@__HAN__ Please stop using our hashtag to serve your own needs. Your performative activism is harmful to what we're trying to do and is making our work visible in ways we are trying to avoid.

@KirstieKares I can't believe this, after all I've done for you and your cause. I've been a feminist so long I feel like I invented aspects of it.

@__HAN__ Please stop. Please think about what you're doing.

@KirstieKares Stop being so rude. I'm doing my best and am here to learn and grow.

@__HAN__ Please. We have done nothing but say please and have endured your self-serving behaviour long enough.

@KirstieKares Fine. I just think we need to get activism back to Kits.

Kirstie leaves the private message and posts once.

@KirstieKares
Every neighbourhood needs help, even ones that seem shiny and healthy on the outside.

Kirstie mutes her own chirp and puts her phone down. Tomorrow is a big day. She needs to be rested.

She tries to fall asleep, but memories of her activist past flash in her mind. The time she suggested they all wear leopard catsuits to counter-protest the anti-abortion protesters, and everyone laughed at her. When she climbed onto a cardboard box to get everyone's attention at the climate change meeting and fell through it, ripping her cargo pants and scraping both her knees, and then she got an infection from stumbling, knee cuts first, into mouse shit no one had cleaned up. That one evening she told everyone they were stupid for not understanding the nuances of her sixty-four-step plan for the protest against the poli-sci department. How could they be so naive? "I am leading this charge, and you can follow me, or you can fail!" she'd said to them. Maybe she'd yelled. Maybe she'd stomped. Maybe she'd pushed Jessie when she tried to calm Kirstie down.

Weeks after missing the protest, Kirstie avoided everyone. Went to the cafeteria at off-peak hours. Spent her meal plan points on protein bars so she could leave her room as infrequently as possible while still getting as much protein as possible. She wrote all her thoughts in her tablet journal, intended for no one's eyes but hers and without any hashtags to draw people in.

*None of these people know how much I'll be able to achieve.
*They'll all be sorry that I'm gone.
*Who will help them now?
*To live morally is to be hated, even by those you feel closest to.
*I miss my boy band posters.

Finally, one of the other activist students came by her room and told her that they'd felt she wasn't taking the cause seriously. That she'd spent too much time on her multi-step plan rather than logistics, that she cared more about what they wore to protest than what they were protesting. They'd held entire meetings without her. Not just without her but about her, behind her back. Then they'd protested without her.

She started grad school the next September, and soon after, she got work, dropped out of school, and quickly bought her own place. Even now, to fall asleep at night, she searches for the other student activists online to see who looks more miserable and less successful than her. That seems to be most of them. This always soothes her enough to get some rest.

She wakes up early and tells her robot blinds to open. The sun shines in, illuminating her bed. There is a light haze over the mountains. A mild smoky day. Her phone pings, and she springs up. It's a new email from the group. A blind cc'd message.

> Okay, plans have changed for your group. I can't say too much, but I need you to show up this morning at a different location. I know, I know. But we're spreading out and will come together eventually. Go to the middle of Georgia and Burrard and stake out the middle of the street. We'll all be at other big intersections. And then we'll come together. I promise it'll work. —Ang

She jumps out of bed and rushes to the bathroom for a quick morning pee. Then to the kitchen, where she stands at the island, unpacking the ingredients of her meal prep kit. The one she prefers is Whole Original Keto FOD Organic Forever, or WOKFOF. Though, by the time she gets to the fifth meal in the kit, something has always gone off. Today, it's the sunflower seeds, which usually give a nice added crunch when the dressing is so minimal, but she won't miss them in her salad today because it has kale, her favourite. She loves kale so much that Lila once got her a card that read, "Kale yeah! It's your birthday!" which she keeps on her fridge with a magnet of a leaf of kale doing yoga, another perfect gift from Coral.

As she mixes the minimal dressing, her Apple Watch starts going off, pinging and pinging, the notification noise for ZChirp. She stops to check. She's lost twenty-five followers. No replies. No engagements. But it doesn't matter. Ang gave her the new instructions. Last-minute changes are something she rolls with at work all the time. Han might not like her, but she's going to be there to support everyone. Including herself. She's been letting her activism fall by the wayside for too long.

She blasts a smoothie in her Vitamix and adds extra protein. After her smoothie and salad, she showers, taking extra time to wash her long hair so she can more easily manipulate it into the perfect bun on top of her head. Just like after a yoga class. Then she puts on her new black yoga pants, a black fleece jacket, and a slim black running toque. She looks at herself in the mirror. Modern revolutionary chic. She is everything, she is ready, she is exceptional.

They're supposed to communicate using only an app that can't be tracked or hacked. She has it installed on her phone, but it's oddly silent. She was told everyone would be active on it first thing in the morning, right at the crack of rush hour. On the app, she fires off a message of encouragement to Ang, but it won't go through. "WE GOT THIS! ♡✊" just stares back at her as if she's sent the message to herself.

She parks her car in the secure EasyPark lot. Car thefts are way too common downtown, but she needs to be close to the action. Walking through the city centre, she breathes confidence with each step. At the appointed corner, she looks around. No one else is there yet. According to her phone, she's right on time. Exactly ten minutes early. Maybe everyone else is having a hard time getting in. Maybe the train is down. Maybe her group is small.

The instructions were to just go, not to wait. People will join. That's the plan. She tightens her shoelaces and steps into the street. Cars are speeding by. People are shouting at her, honking. She's called a "crazy bitch," a "psycho," there's a lot of "Holy fuck, get out of the way!" Breathe, move, stay strong. Years of yoga have prepared her for a moment like this, for this exact moment, in fact. In the centre of the road, she stands, her core strong, her posture perfect. She holds up her hand-painted "Feminists for Change" sign and looks over at the mountains obscured by early morning mist and that ring of smoke. People continue shouting, honking, threatening to call the police.

She checks her phone again. No messages. She opens ZChirp and types in the hashtag. Nothing posted. She goes to Han's feed but sees only a blue padlock. She's been blocked. Cars scream past her. She checks Ang's feed. There are photos of everyone standing on the bridge at the other end of the downtown peninsula, blocking traffic in both directions. They've hung a huge banner over the side. They have outlined a list of demands. They're all together. An SUV narrowly swerves to avoid her. The shouting and honking are like a low buzz now. Someone throws a coffee cup out the window, and when it hits her chest, the coffee explodes. Cold coffee, with real dairy creamer in it. She gags, spits. Dripping wet, she opens her camera app, grips her sign to her chest, and takes a selfie.

Holding out her poster like a stop sign, she works to get out of the intersection, shouting at vehicles. "Excuse me! I am a woman and a pedestrian! Please do not hit me with your cheap sedan!"

On the sidewalk, people are staring at her. This was the plan all along. To get her to understand her own power. It all makes sense. Kirstie needed to go through this to become resilient, a force. She runs the photo through all her filter apps and then posts it to ZChirp with #GoingItAloneForFeminism. She'll find more people, and she'll lead them herself. As she's always been destined to do. She's ready.

Empty cans rattle in her bag. School started fifteen minutes ago, and the recycling depot opens in thirty minutes. At Main and East 2nd, she hops off the bus, wanders through the old industrial district. Here too there are condos, designer chocolatiers, beers that cost more than her mom makes per hour. The mountains look bright. The spring rain down here means fresh dust on the peaks. The older woman at the recycling depot smiles at her. She tells the woman the spray paint was for a school project, a mural spreading awareness. Of what, she doesn't say. Just those words. *School. Project. Awareness.* They give her a sheen of legitimacy. The woman takes the cans, hands her some coins.

DREAM ON

The sky is pink, rust, and grey, a colour palette that was popular this spring for makeup, clothes, shoes, and every manner of accessory. Once summer rolled around, influencers were saying that designers were looking to the sky, wanting everything to be heightened, literally. That the trending colours were a comment on the increasingly charred landscape and surrounding atmosphere.

It's deep into August, and this fire season has been the longest yet. Since most people are staying inside or wearing masks, lipstick sales have dropped significantly. The industry is desperate for someone to convince people to buy more. If you can't gallivant around a summer patio in a fresh shade for selfies, it's just not quite summer. At least that's what Hazel was screaming into my texts this morning.

I turn from the window and try to find the best spot to set up for today's event. Last time, I used my closet as a backdrop, and the time before, the tapestry behind my kitchen table. For my solo videos, I have my bedroom studio, but I haven't quite decided how to present myself when I'm with Hazel, so I'll mix it up every time, I guess. I can use a pair of palazzo pants draped and pinned on a board, plants as dressing, and the ring light does the rest of the work.

Hazel is a lifestyle interpreter. Though she hates the word *influencer*, because she isn't influencing so much as interpreting what's going on. "Bringing what I see to my viewers, my fans, in a way they can understand and feel connected to. I'm interpreting trends, styles, vibes."

I'm just starting out, but *influencer* feels right to me. I'm finding my place, practising, learning. It's nice to have a mentor, someone who's been at this for almost ten years.

I check my makeup and hair, spritz the crown of my head with some saltwater spray. It's one of the products I was sent to use this week, but it's so hard to show the result. I guess that's the challenge. To make something exciting and desirable out of what mostly looks like nothing.

Once I've moved the pothos into place and tacked up the floral fabric, making sure to get the pants' wide legs but not the elastic waistband into the shot behind me, I place my chair and table in position. We aren't going live for another fifteen minutes, so I've got time to scroll.

I open app after app. Images from the recent fires are everywhere. They've been blowing in from the Interior, the mountains to the north, the south, essentially every corner. Videos show thick smoke curling around towns, dark patches on mountainsides where trees used to be. The sunsets are horribly beautiful, apocalyptic and a little scary. #WorldInFlames is trending, and I go through the top posts. Lots of those tragic gorgeous sunsets, empty city streets with a red orb of a sun between concrete buildings, children in tiny haz-mat suits swimming in inflatable pools with burning forests behind them.

The top trending story is still the same: #NeonFlame. A popular influencer, Neon, was doing yoga on a mountaintop, right near a forest edge that was burning quickly. The person filming her tried to convince her to move, to not do the shoot. In the video that was leaked, you can hear Neon saying, “Are you fucking stupid? We can’t miss an opportunity like this. Now, move to the left, get me from this side. My calves are gonna glow in this light. No, fucking move this way!” Then a charred branch falls down on her, and she catches fire for a moment. The whole thing was caught on camera, her running around, the person filming screaming for her to roll on the goddamn ground.

The video was released in two cuts. One at regular speed and one in slow motion. Neon assumed the cameraman leaked it and is suing him for more money than either of them is worth, but it became a viral sensation when she also posted it herself. “I am reclaiming my tragedy! Because I’m a survivor!” She added an intro, describing the lessons she learned from briefly being on fire: She felt closer to nature, had more understanding of mortality, and a light was lit within her to raise awareness about forest fires. She’s now selling T-shirts with an illustration of her in flames and text that reads “Set Your Intentions. Set Your Soul Ablaze!”

A reminder pops into my view of Neon’s feed, and I lock my phone into the tripod and get in place to start the video.

Hazel’s energy seems a little low as we start the live stream. I reach into my brain bag of tricks.

“Well, Hazel, you’re looking more gorgeous than ever. I’d love to hear about this new glow you’ve got! Give us the deets,” I say, raising a perfectly Glossiered eyebrow.

Hazel sparks up and launches into a ten-minute talk on the three types of skin spreads and highlighters she’s using.

“Thanks, Pet. I do want to say that we are of course thinking about everyone affected by the fires right now. So serious. So sad. So scorched.”

“Yes, of course.”

"And to Neon, we're thinking of you. Take care. Light and love."

"Yes, love you, Neon! And love to you, my Hazel. Thank you so much for tuning in. We love to collab, my babies. And we'll see you next month. Don't forget to like and subscribe to my EverEverStream. Bye and take care, my beautiful ones!"

I close the app. Immediately, a call comes in from Hazel. She likes to debrief via FaceTime after our ImageScroller Live has ended.

"OMG, I am so jealous. Fucking Neon. I wish I'd catch on fire. Do you know how many clicks I'd get? How many likes? That's, like, so many sponsorships. I wouldn't want to really damage my skin, though, especially my face." She has already thrown her hair into a messy bun and put on an old denim shirt over her tight white mock neck.

"Hazel! No one wants to be on fire."

"Well, you know what I mean."

She sighs, leans into the camera, and pulls off her fake eyelashes. I can see the crow's feet at the edges of her eyes. She's got the most expensive skin care money can buy—though she gets it for free—and looks great. But there are cracks. She's aging, though well and with help.

"Are you doing okay?" I ask.

"Just a bit tired."

"Yeah, I kind of noticed you were a bit low when we started up."

She scowls. "Excuse me? I was fine. Great as always," she says, glaring into the phone.

"Oh sorry, I didn't mean anything. I just want to make sure you're okay. That's all."

She walks out of frame, starts throwing clothes into a pile on the bed. I can see strips of fabric flying closer and closer to the screen. Without coming back to the camera, she shouts, "'Kay, I've gotta go get ready. Bye!"

Then her finger pops into view and she's gone.

I've been at this for a year, and I'm doing okay, but others who started around the same time have already surpassed me in followers and sponsorships. The guy with the hamster co-host has a TV deal with ISC, the Influencer Shopping Channel. He started out talking pet food and now he has an entire line of hamster athleisure. I started to make just enough to get by a few months ago, so I quit my barista job to focus on doing this full-time. I moved across the country at eighteen, ready to live that West Coast lifestyle. Hiking, park exercise in designer yoga pants, sitting on patios. But the smoke has made almost all outdoor activities when it's not raining completely unfun and unglamorous.

I don't make enough to go out and be seen. I rarely get clothes, and if I do, I can't be seen in them twice. More importantly, I'm not important enough to be invited places. Last month, I got an invitation to the launch of an artisanal douche, but going to events for products that don't showcase your face isn't exactly the smartest move. I did pose next to the Flower Folds mascot, a plush vagina with perfume atomizers for hands. So far it hasn't resulted in any additional revenue, and the swag bag was mostly undercarriage scents that gave me a rash. This month, I might not make enough for rent. Food seems like a luxury. But the only closet in my place is filled to the brim with free products I could possibly sell, if it comes to that. It's not the best look to be selling slightly used skincare, but I can't say I won't do it.

In today's mail, I got a new product that I'm excited about: a day-of-the-week eyeshadow palette with special stickers to put on your eyelids, so when you wink it shows which day it is. I swipe the Wildcat Wednesday orange over my right lid. Applying the sticker is harder than it looks, though, and there's only one of each. After flubbing it half a dozen times, I open my portable brow kit and grab the smallest tweezer I own. My eye is twitching from too many false starts, but I steady my hand and manage to get the sticker on. I finish my eye with burnt liner and lashes, add a nude lip, dab on a little blush. A little bit Glossier, a little bit mod.

The sky outside has gotten a little less smoky, and from down the alley you can see the tip of the mountain for the first time in weeks. It's glowing orange, almost matching my eyeshadow. I grab my lightweight tripod and remote. In the alley, I pose as if no one is watching, even though there are open blinds all over the place. People are sitting on their patios wearing masks, or with Plexiglas walls that convert their patios into pseudo-sunrooms. I pout, I smile, but in every close-up I wink to show that Wednesday right eye. I cough a few times, find it easier to inhale through my nose. There's still smoke in the air, despite it looking clearer.

The pictures turn out well, and I post a carousel of photos on ImageScroller. If you swipe through them, it looks like a stop-motion film. I hashtag the brand, #WildcatWednesday, a few of my personal ones (#PetLoves, #PetraLovesYou, #BrandPet), and of course, #ad. #PetLoves always brings in additional followers looking for pet content who are surprised to enjoy my feed. Except the few who berate me for "robbing them of quality cat videos, you narcissistic bitch!"

Checking through my DMs, I notice several new message requests. I decline them all—they're either bots, creeps, creepy bots, or girls I knew in high school who'd shout "SLUT!" at me for wearing a dress and not jeans. Now they want to tell me how excited they are for me and also hey can they get some free fifty-dollar lipsticks? Delete, delete, delete.

There's one new message from a local organically sourced vegan makeup brand, Skin So You.

@SkinSoYou Dear Petra,
We are big fans of yours. Thank you so much for all you've been doing. We love your collaborations with Hazel, and your videos feel genuine.

Please call us to arrange a meeting. We have a unique opportunity for you.

Roz

Marketing Manager

Skin So You

604-555-4440

At first, it looks like a form letter or spam. And why wouldn't my videos seem genuine? I'm not like the other girls; I say what I mean, and even if I don't like a product, I'm truthful but never cruel. I wish I could be sometimes, but it's hard to shit on free things.

The message is two minutes old. Sent right after I posted the Wildcat Wednesday photos. They've already liked the post. And left a comment: "Love to see your innovative self!"

Phone calls are basically unheard of, but they asked me to call, so after some deep breathing exercises, I do.

"Hello, Skin So You, how may we help you find your best self?"

"Hi, I'm looking for Roz."

"Do you have an appointment?"

"No, she left me a DM?"

"Name?"

"Petra. My ImageScroller handle is PetraSoFine."

"Hold one moment, please."

The sounds of a waterfall rush through my phone speaker. Then someone laughs before saying, "Hello, Roz here. Who am I speaking with?"

"Hello, It's Petra. You just sent me a DM on ImageScroller?"

"Oh yes, yes, yes. Thrilled to have you on the line. Listen, this is best handled in person, not over the phone. Can you come in? Everyone here wants to meet you. Is tomorrow good? Because it's great for us!"

I see myself reflected in the mirrored doors of the office tower. There was a smoke advisory alert this morning, so I'm masked up. I have a tiny face. The only mask I can get to fit is child's size and covered in cartoon bears from some new TV show I've never heard of. And it's pink. I'm wearing ripped jeans, a cropped tee, and a long drop-shouldered cardigan to make the whole look a bit edgier. Something I would wear regularly for sponcon, sponsored content. Which is most of my feed now. Rarely do I post fun shots of me and any friends, mostly because that's really just Hazel. And the one girl from the coffee shop who doesn't live in the suburbs and occasionally invites me to 1980s nights at the bar that used to be primarily queer but now seems full of university undergrads every night.

I take the elevator up to the twenty-eighth floor. At the entrance, I'm given a visitor's badge and asked if I want my mask cleaned. They offer that service. I decline and shove it into my purse. Then I'm guided to a large office where two women and an older man sit across the table. They get up and gush as I walk in, cooing and oohing, then sit back down, and I'm still standing there, clutching my bag. They begin speaking in sequence, as if this is a rehearsed play.

FIRST WOMAN: Thank you for meeting us. A real thrill.

SECOND WOMAN: Thrilling.

MAN: Just thriller-diller!

FIRST WOMAN: Now, we want to pay you a lot of money to test out something new.

SECOND WOMAN: This is very different and special and new.

MAN: And the product isn't quite what you might think.

ME: Oh, I love testing new products. I've never been invited in for an official meeting before, just to test new products.

FIRST WOMAN: It's a thrilling new product.

(They all nod.)

ME: Okay.

FIRST WOMAN: Well, it's less of a product and more of a procedure.

(I gulp down some water.)

SECOND WOMAN: Now, hear us out.

MAN: This is something that's never been done in the beauty industry before.

FIRST WOMAN: Have you ever wanted to change your facial features?

SECOND WOMAN: Maybe you wish you could adjust your nose, your eyes, your cheekbones? Like Mr. Potato Head?

FIRST WOMAN: Like Mrs. Potato Head.

SECOND WOMAN: Like Ms. Potato Head.

MAN: Like Mx. Potato Head.

FIRST WOMAN: Really more like the ability to Photoshop your own face.

SECOND WOMAN: Your face is known, but not well known. Not yet. So it's the perfect face to adapt.

MAN: To launch our product.

ME: You want my face, but you don't want my face?

FIRST WOMAN: Precisely.

SECOND WOMAN: You're as sharp as you are pretty.

MAN: A great influencer asset.

FIRST WOMAN: Think about it.

SECOND WOMAN: Let us know.

MAN: By Saturday night.

FIRST WOMAN: At the latest.

SECOND WOMAN: We want to move forward with a fall release. It's already going to be written up in the September issue. And if we can get photos just before that.

MAN: Well, then we'll really be cooking with gas.

They sent me home with a hundred-page glossy booklet that explains the procedure in graphic detail. It includes health and safety information, as well as a twenty-page NDA and a ten-page agreement and media contract. They are not liable if I die under the knife. I have two days to make a decision. And tomorrow, if I want, I can book a video session with their surgeon, who will walk me through everything. It's a lot of money. More than I imagined. More than enough to live on for several years. And it's not exclusive. I can still promote other brands.

"It might even enhance, ahem, your other brand opportunities," the Second Woman said.

I text Hazel that I might have some news. She responds with a thumbs-up emoji and a question-mark reaction. But I can't tell her yet, I have to wait. I say I'll let her know when I know.

I decide to read through the booklet again and sleep on it. I can call the doctor in the morning. In bed, I turn on my ring light. My hair looks perfectly tousled. I take a casual selfie with my hair cascading over the pillow, a rare opportunity to post what I want, just a photo of me. My caption: "New waves of opportunity could be on the horizon!"

The doctor has the most intense office I've ever seen. Black lights everywhere, neon signs, a disco ball desk lamp, throbbing bass over the speakers. Like a club for cosmetic surgeons.

"Have you had a chance to look over the brochure?"

As if this is a relaxing spa vacation I'm going to take for my health.

"I have. I guess I do have some technical questions."

"Shoot." He throws fingers guns at me and leans back in his chair.

"I want to know how this will actually work."

"I'm going to need you to be more specific."

"Sorry, it's hard to focus." I gesture to the room in general.

He changes the light pattern on the disco lamp to a more subtle pulse and lowers the volume of the music.

I lean forward, realize I'm slouching, and adjust my posture. "The brochure was actually pretty specific, so *technical* isn't the right word, but I want to know how I'll feel. How long will I be under? Will I be able to communicate with people afterward? When will my mouth and eyes work again? Will I be able to breathe normally?"

He hits a button on his desk and shuts everything down.

"Okay. I see. I thought you were young and adventurous. You're young and serious. We can work with this. You'll be able to see right away, but it'll be cloudy. Your mouth will work, but imagine you've had four intense dental surgeries at once. As mentioned in the brochure, the Replacement Features will be provided in special packaging. Do not attempt to use them for at least two weeks. This is also mentioned on the packaging."

"That's good to know. Um, also, can I eat?"

"Not the traditional way. We'll provide you with a special tube, and liquid meals will be delivered for those two weeks. They're very high in protein. Whole30, keto style. Everyone is doing intermittent fasting now anyway. Right?"

He's not wrong. And I do take care with what I eat to maintain my influencer weight goals. I stare into the unlit disco ball on his desk. My face is average at best. I'm genetically lucky, naturally thin with good cheekbones, clear skin, and a high hairline that really lets me show my face. I know some people who will shave their hairlines just to get a little more forehead framing for a single campaign.

"Listen. I know it's a lot to consider. But you'll be on the forefront of a beauty trend that is going to soar. Seriously. This is the future. And the attention you'll get just from the publicity for the procedure? You'll be a millionaire in no time. Think of what happened to the first person to get the vampire facelift. That was huge. Everyone was talking about it. And the healing was minimized by weeks. Almost instantaneous. Every glossy and vlog had them on, every morning show. Within a week they were selling the number-one flat-tummy CBD gummies and weight-loss vodka. A revelation."

I blink at my disco ball reflection, so many tiny versions of my face. My current face.

I leave the consult and head straight to the juice bar to meet Hazel. She sent a message that I couldn't answer until I was out of the appointment. She even left voice mails, multiple, which is so unlike her.

"Pet, I just got back from the doctor. Please text me back."

"P, are you around? Did you get some modelling or something? Come on."

"Petra, are you fucking around? Are you fucking normal? Call me. Don't even text. Or just meet me at Juicy J Fit Juice. ASAP."

I walk in and she's cowering in the back of the small space. At the corner table she always says is for people too ashamed to be seen in the front window. Those are the people we want to help to change and grow. Before I even sit down with my celery-wheatgrass-soil smoothie, she's talking at me.

"I have to tell you something. We need to cancel our next few recordings. I'm sick." She's already finished her juice and is now sipping sparkling water through a glass straw. Her lipstick still looks perfect. "There's something in my bloodstream. I have to get more tests, but it could be very bad. I can't work right now. It could be in my heart or my lungs too. I don't know. I have to get tests all the time, and they're making me take this medication that's going to make my face swell to the size of, like, seventeen watermelons."

I sip some juice. It tastes mostly like dirt. "Seventeen watermelons seems like a lot. I bet it won't be that bad."

"I don't know what I'll do. I have stuff, but, like, I won't be able to make money. I don't really get paid that well. It's just shitty. I'm not eighteen anymore. I'm aging out of being interesting."

"No way. You'll always be interesting, no matter your age," I say and reach out to grip her hand.

She holds her glass to her face and starts sobbing into it, then coughs a few times. I motion for her to sip some water. The wildfire smoke can't be helping anyone's condition. The extreme weather warnings are in the deepest red of the index.

"I'm sorry, Haz." I get up and grab a handful of napkins for her, trade her the wad of paper for her water glass.

"They say it could be an allergy or a severe reaction to something. Even, like, poisoning!"

"Poisoning?" I ask, as she blows her nose in the paper napkins.

"Like, they have to test to see if it's from something I've been using. I use so many products, I never really think about it."

"If it's from a product, you could sue. I bet you could sue, Haz."

She slams the table angrily. "If I sue, I'll never be able to interpret again! God, Pet, don't be so naive."

She gets herself a second smoothie, this one all sugar and fruit. I don't finish mine and pour most of it into the compost bin. I can see the smoothie barista flirting with Hazel, who's doing her bashful act. A very older-generation move. When she gets back to the table with her drink, she's smiling.

"Weren't you going to tell me some news?"

"Oh no, it's not important. I mean, not like your health. I don't even know if it's news yet. It's nothing."

I walk Hazel home. At the front of her building, we hug. Her body weight rests on me, and I have to really hold her up. It's the longest hug we've ever had. She turns, not looking back, and with her head down, opens the door and walks into the stairwell. As soon as she's out of sight, I know what I'm going to do. I'll take that money. I'll get the product, procedure, whatever they want to call it. I don't have to tell Hazel we can't do videos together for a while because she also can't do videos. It's easy. It'll be easy.

At home, I electronically sign the contract, the waiver, the NDA, and the promise to never sue, no matter what happens, and then I send in my most current high-res selfies for the doctors to review before the procedure. I can at least help Hazel with some of her expenses while she's off. There's no influencers' union yet, so we don't have medical benefits.

Moments after I send everything in, I receive a notification of the date of the procedure. Less than a week from now. My phone prompts me to add it to my calendar, and I do. There it is, marked in a bold purple rectangle. One half of the payment arrives via e-transfer. I deposit the money. I'll send some to Hazel as soon as the procedure is over, and I'll keep the rest.

I check my spreadsheet to confirm how many posts I have to stock up before next week. I only have to make two sponsored posts, and they're small—each one pays barely enough to be worth it. I'll also need to make sure to have enough regular posts—stories and main feed—that I seem like my regular self, to ensure I stay in the algorithms of my followers. I grab the sponsored products from the shelf, riffle through my closet, and line up several outfits along the bed, trying to decide what I'll look best in while trying to convince people a cream will make their face look younger, even though my face is already young. The doctor said that's why I'm ideal for the procedure. I'll heal better since my skin is more youthful. Something about elastin and scarring. I barely remember now.

I spend all night changing, posing, shifting the light, putting on entirely new makeup looks for every shot. I've got a few days left of the days-of-the-week eyeshadow posts. I save every post, ready for when it needs to be shared. By the time I finish, it's 5 a.m., and I can hear the songbirds outside. Sometimes it almost sounds like they're wheezing too, with the pressure on their tiny lungs from the smoke.

From the kitchen, I grab a handful of baby carrots and cucumbers, a bag of SmartPop!, and a bottle of sparkling wine. I put on an episode of *Friends*, let it soothe me in the background while I sip and scroll through photos of other people in their homes. So many people paid to do something besides posting their photos online.

On the day of the procedure, I come in with the tote I've packed, wearing my loosest sweatpants. Before I even say hello, I'm whisked to the procedure room.

"You're late." The doctor is furious.

I check my phone, and it's clearly fifteen minutes before the scheduled time. "Excuse me?"

"You're late. You were supposed to be here an hour ago, for prep."

"That's not the message I received."

A nurse, or someone I assume is a nurse, takes my bag and jacket and hands me a plastic basket filled with what look like tiny beauty samples.

"Well, I guess you didn't get the right message. Now I'm in a rush. If we can get you out of these clothes and get your face scrubbed with these poultices and serums and whatever else is in this basket in the next ten minutes, everything will still be fine. I'll also be doing a quick chemical peel on you."

I stand and let the nurse take off my clothes, put them in a bag, and toss it into a cupboard with my other belongings. She holds out a gown and I step into it, then she motions for me to go into the bathroom, where I wash my face with every item in the basket. Drying my face with a hand towel, I try to give myself a good look. It's what I see every day in the mirror and in photos. I'm so used to looking at it, but this is the last time I'll see it this way. I slap a palm to my forehead. It's fine. For the best. Anyone can change, and today that will be me.

The nurse bursts through the door and leads me by the arm back to the procedure room. There's a long table for me to lie on, and I do. A bright light glows above me. The doctor is wearing a protective face shield, and his rubber gloves look sparkly. I can see my face reflected over his in the clear plastic of his face guard. An amalgam of our features, my eyes just below his eyes, my nose on top of his, my mouth below his and fuller, his like the lips of a badger. I wish I had taken one more selfie today. But there are already so many images of me.

They place a mask over my nose and mouth, and the doctor doesn't even ask me to count down backward before I'm out.

The sky is orange and black. I feel like I'm inside a piece of sticky Halloween candy. I'm at the beach, but it's so dark I can barely see the water, the mountains, the sky. I can hear seagulls screaming. Crows are dive-bombing people near me, and then the birds and people seem to disappear. My hands are heavy—I try to swat away the birds and smoke, but I can barely lift them. Instead, I start running toward the old blue bathhouse. When I walk through the bathroom door, it's not like I remember it. There are mirrors everywhere. On the floor, the ceiling, and every stall door. I can't see my own face. It's a hazy form that seems to change shape every time I look in a different mirror. I have to pee so badly. I grab my crotch and scuttle to a stall. As soon as I open the stall door, I'm immediately somewhere else.

Everything is salmon pink, and a raspberry smoke wafts away to reveal a sixty-inch television. A show I used to love as a kid is playing, a sitcom about married people that I was too young to understand. I liked the quirky neighbour and her two dogs. Then, in the TV, I see Hazel. She's thin and her face is smoky. We can't seem to talk to each other, but we know we're together, and everything feels dangerous. She's slowly disappearing, like a candle burning out. I reach out for her and touch the screen. My heavy hand smashes through.

I wake up and touch my face. I don't know which parts of me are where, and I barely remember where I am. A sitcom from my childhood plays on the small tablet on the table beside my hospital bed, and the laugh track feels like it's for me. I tap the screen. The time is 2:08 a.m. The air conditioning is severe; in this room you'd never know fire is ravaging the outside world. I pull the sheets up, wishing I had a second blanket. I've got five more hours to rest before they send me home with multiple parts for a whole new face.

I lied to the doctor, told him I had someone at home waiting. Signed another waiver confirming it. They send me home with a swag bag of medical ephemera. Creams, painkillers, vitamins, a pillow that fits around my face to keep me from leaning too much on one side or the other, and some free pink T-shirts and tank tops with the name of the clinic printed on them. There are more care instructions in a booklet. Everything is stuffed into a small plastic tote bag, which I cram into my larger tote before I leave.

I'm supposed to have an exit meeting, but the doctor had to fly to Brazil immediately after he finished, so he made me a video from the plane that I'm supposed to watch as soon as I get home.

I get into the VoltaShare I prebooked and they're playing Rihanna, which I take to be a good omen. Through my bandages, I watch the morning come into focus. The smoke is low, and there's ash on the store awnings, on the sidewalk. You can see it blowing around in the sky. I'm not allowed to wear a mask, because it won't allow the procedure to set properly, so I cover my mouth as I get up and walk up to my apartment alone.

Inside, the hallway is crowded with a tiny fridge blocking the bathroom door, boxes of shake mix packets, and a few different types of long feeding straws. I gave a copy of my keys to the clinic so they could supposedly set everything up before I got home.

My face hurts, burns, but I decide to move things around so I can at least pee. There's not much in the cupboards, so the food and straws fit easily into the one I usually keep for low-calorie snacks. I wheel the fridge over, and it fits neatly between the edge of the small couch and my two-person kitchen table, and luckily that's where the outlet is located. I plug it back in and sit on the floor, panting. Facial features look out at me from behind the glass door. It looks like a bit like a wine fridge, but instead of rosés and whites, it's noses and lips and cheeks in individual glass jars. The fridge slides open like a bottom-drawer freezer. Each jar has a sealed top marked with a description in Sharpie. It's like looking at a series of lipsticks, but instead of creative shades, they're named for the classic celebrities whom these features are modelled after. Some are too generic; I can't tell if "Jennifer" is Garner or Aniston or someone else. And so many of those people got rid of their original noses. They made changes. Look at their careers.

Even though it's early morning and I was passed out all night, I'm exhausted from moving the fridge and the boxes. I change into a clean tank top and crawl into bed.

I wake up an hour later, curled in a ball. They told me to sleep flat on my back, but I'm a fetal position sleeper, and I can't stop myself from rolling over. I remember the pillow I'm supposed to wear and the video I'm supposed to watch. And the painkillers at the bottom of my bag.

I get up, collect everything, and get back in. I adjust the pillow on my face, take two painkillers, and fire up the video.

"Petra. You should now be at home, safely being cared for. This is like any other surgery—you will need to rest as much as possible. Especially as you're expected to send us proof of your facial options via photo in exactly three weeks.

"Here is some advice: Cover your mirrors. Don't look at yourself for at least a week. Keep the bandages on. And then, don't pay too much attention. Eat three times a day, even if you're not hungry. Do not get addicted to the painkillers. Apply the salve five times a day. Wash with the cloths provided and then dispose of them. Do not reuse. That's all.

"If you have questions, the emergency clinic number is on the back of the care brochure. But, mostly just rest. I've injected you with multiple serums that will boost healing. And don't even think about taking any alternative medicines, okay? We need chemicals, girl.

"Okay, gotta get off the plane. Rest up!"

I get back up and toss a blanket over the full-length mirror beside the closet. Then grab some towels from inside. The bedroom is dark. I couldn't look at myself even if I wanted to. In the bathroom, I keep the lights off and toss a towel over the mirror, but not without catching a glimpse of my bandaged face. I reach a finger inside my mouth and briefly touch what feels like jelly where my lips should be. I whimper, drop my hand, and get back into bed.

I'd set up my bedroom for what I thought would be maximum relaxation, but it's cluttered, and I feel hemmed in. I moved the TV from the living room to the wall opposite my headboard and added piles of extra blankets to the bed in case I get a chill, as I was told I might. But I also put two fans on either side of the bed in case it gets too hot or the smoke starts to seep in. The windows in this building are single paned, and I often wake up smelling strong smoke even when I've shut them all.

I'm allowed to remove the bandages today. I'm supposed to. I need to send a progress report and photos. It's been a week and it'll be the first time I've looked in the mirror. But when I get to the bathroom, I can't bring myself to remove the towel. I just stand there in the dark.

I crawl back into my nest in bed and remove the bandages, unwinding each one and dropping it onto the plastic backing from a food packet. I turn on the ring light, turn my head to the bedside table, close my eyes, and take as many selfies as I can.

Without looking at the photos, I send them to the doctor and the executives, using the secure VPN, as instructed. Then I take two more painkillers and a sleeping pill.

An hour later, I'm still in pain, awake, and checking my email every two seconds for a response. They've barely communicated with me other than to ensure I've received deliveries of the food packets. I scroll through ImageScroller intermittently. Other influencers are leaning into summer. Pool shoots, highlighter with green gardens as backdrops, sailboats and sandals for home pedicure kits. None of them ever do their own nails, but it's good to make it look like anyone could do it.

A few months ago, Hazel asked if I had any rivals, and I said no. I hadn't even thought about it. Mostly because things change so quickly it's hard to keep up, even for someone who's online all the time.

"I guess I've tried to take a little something from everyone. To learn that way," I answered.

"Huge mistake. You don't want to mimic, you want to do the opposite. Pick a rival and do the opposite of whatever they do. If they only do a certain kind of photo, then you never do that photo. Even if it means they favour one side of their face or they use the same backdrop all the time."

That was when I started to use different backdrops. Trying to change it up every time, to make it look like I was going places, being seen, gaining access to things people want.

I go to Hazel's profile. She's posted a #TBT of some outtakes from her early work. She always shows a little of the "off" side, which is why we work well together. It's a carousel of photos: one is blurry, unfocused, and in another, a slash of light cuts across her face, bisecting it. She's beautiful.

An alert pops up, and I swipe for it.

> We love the progress. Keep resting! More food coming on Thursday. We're almost there! We are so close! Stay on track!

"We're almost there." *We.*

I plug my phone back in and close my eyes. If I could sleep away the next week, that would be ideal. I just want this part to be over.

I hear my phone bleat—Hazel trying to FaceTime. I decline the call. I miss her. I have barely spoken at all, and I'm worried I'll sound different. I've been responding to her texts sporadically. Spending the past week in bed, taking pills, and sleeping as much as possible has been the only way to make it through. I'm groggy, bleary, but I can see she's tried to call at least four times today. It's after 1:00 p.m. I can't tell the time with the blackout curtains closed.

It's been two weeks since the procedure, and although I've been posting regularly, I haven't responded to any messages. My brain is foggy, and it's hard to be engaged. Human interaction would be great right now, but I can't bring myself to answer questions about why a filmy milk will add collagen to your skin. All I want to do is sleep.

I'm in less pain, but there are burning twinges that seem to flare up whenever I eat anything with flavour. It's hard to say if these things are connected. Maybe the sucking motion of eating is making my facial muscles engage in a way that's dangerous.

Hazel calls again. I pick up the phone and set it beside me, pointed away from my face.

"Petra, are you there?"

"Hi. I'm sorry. I should have been checking in on you. I know you were going in for more tests last week."

"Yeah, thank you. I really was, like, does she even care about me?"

I turn my face and wince. "Of course I do. I really do. How are you? How did the tests go?"

"I don't know yet. Still have to go for more. I'm on a weird diet. But I feel okay. Just need to confirm it's not some permanent damage. Hey, what are you doing? Why isn't the phone facing you? Are you with someone?"

"Oh no, I just don't look very good right now."

"Oh my God, stop. You have never not looked incredible." My "lip" is trembling, and I start to cry. "Are you okay? What is going on?"

"I don't want to tell you. This should be about you. You're the one who has serious health issues." I can't talk anymore, I'm sobbing too much.

"I will come straight over there if you don't tell me what's happening."

I pick up my phone and raise it to my face.

"Petra, seriously, I can't even see you. Why are you crying?"

I close my eyes and turn on the ring light. Hazel screams.

"What the fuck happened to your face? Were you in an accident? I think I'm—"

She drops her phone and runs out of the room. The sounds of vomiting are loud and clear. I turn off the ring light and put my phone down. When Hazel returns, I can tell she's glad my face is nowhere to be seen.

"Holy shit. Sorry. I am just very worried about you."

"I can explain. It's a beauty procedure. I'm being paid for this. More spon."

"Excuse me? What are you even telling me?"

"I'm being paid. It's very cutting edge!"

"Whoever did this to you needs to be put in a maximum-security insane asylum!"

"Hazel, it's for my career. For our careers."

"Why didn't you tell me about this? Because I would have told you to not do it. And the fact you didn't talk to me—well, that's offensive. We're partners!"

I pick up the phone again, forgetting about my face. "It won't look like this forever. It's going to be incredible. I swear. And I've got money for you. So, if you need treatment, you don't have to worry about working. I can help."

"I can't look at you. I have to go. I can't believe you did this."

She hangs up. I throw my phone against the wall, and it lands in a pile of dirty laundry.

An alert goes off. I open my eyes. Today is the day. It's time.

> Petra! Please do the test adjustment as soon as possible. Mornings are best for the face, less likely to have become tight or dirty. But do wash your face first. Do it within the hour. Once we get the photos, we'll send the last update. And if everything goes well, you'll get your final payment and we'll have really achieved something.

I get up and shower, the towel still on the bathroom mirror. I step back from the stream so I can spot wash my face. It doesn't sting anymore, and I'm grateful I can spread some regular face wash over it and not have to use the sticky serums that smell like muscle cream. I realize I haven't washed my hair since I got home and scrub it twice.

When I get out, I stand naked in front of the mirror, my hair up in a towel. My hand feels heavy, and I am trembling. I lower my head, close my eyes, reach up and pull down the towel. I open my eyes and see my toes, same as they ever were, at the bottom of my legs. I glance upward, take a moment to appreciate the rest of my body. When I finally am facing the mirror, it's almost comical. The place where my natural nose used to fit—or, well, still does if I choose to wear it—is a horrible triangular hollow. A basic attempt at carving a jack-o'-lantern. The divots in my face are like a cartoon drawing of Swiss cheese. I don't recognize any part of this face. My mouth is dropped open, but there's no sound coming out. My lips are missing. I'm screaming, but I'm not screaming. My eyes are swollen and red even though they are my eyes, the only thing that still somewhat resembles me.

I run out of the bathroom and open the fridge. Pull out one of each face part without checking which they are. I set them on the counter, grab a bag of ice the company had couriered over from 7-Eleven, pour it into the sink as per the instructions, and place the face pieces in the ice. I can't leave them out of the fridge or off my face for more than twenty minutes, or they'll begin a rotting process, like a ripe banana, but more rapid. I go back to the fridge and get the moulding paste, something so high tech it's barely been approved to be near human skin.

My hands are shaky, but I manage to open the nose jar. I try to get the nose piece to slide into place, but it keeps falling into the sink. I can't stop crying, but without my cheek inserts, the tears drop straight through where firm tissue used to be. I finally let out a loud screech, which oddly calms me. I tell myself this is just like doing elaborate eye makeup, applying individual spidery lashes. Just like Hazel taught me: Use a steady hand, there doesn't have to be a flourish, and the look will speak for itself. I hope she'll want to talk to me again.

I move slowly, no need to race. Each piece takes effort, but the moulding paste works. Though who knows if it'll stay in place when I'm not staying stark still. My hands are still my hands. They take out features, cleanse them, apply paste, and set them in place. I finally manage to adjust everything correctly. I can barely handle looking at myself in the mirror. I can't stop thinking I look like I'm a child's first drawing come to life. A patchwork mess. But this is just the first try—surely it won't be like this forever. They used the word *adjustment*. This is an adjustment period.

I shuffle from the bathroom to the bedroom, where the camera and ring light are set up in the corner, careful not to disrupt anything. Makeup free, with clean skin. That was the request. Without the usual care I take photos with, I stare straight ahead and click the remote, turn to the right, click the remote, turn to the left, click. No editing, no captions, no instant likes.

I transfer the files to a secure server using the VPN, as always. Frozen, I sit and stare at my phone.

After an hour, I get up to stretch and realize I need to pee. When I get back to the bedroom, I pull up the blinds for the first time in weeks. It's so dark I can barely see the apartment buildings at the end of the block. Everything looks covered in soot. There is a crimson strip barely visible through the haze of clouds. The fire is so much closer than before—I feel like I could reach out and push a hand into the dense smoke.

A notification goes off, and I jump for my phone. As I land on my bed, a cheek flies under my pillow. I grab it and try to press it back into place without looking. Then I take a deep breath and open the message.

> Petra, thank you so much for your service. This has been an experimental time. Unfortunately, it looks like these aren't the results we were hoping for. Now, instead of the second payment being made to you, we're going to give you a voucher. This way you can choose to use it to have one of the doctors return your face to its original and beautiful state. Or any of our other procedures. Thank you for this. And again, please don't forget you signed an NDA.

I get up and open the window. Even though the air is toxic, I need to breathe something in, even though this nose is barely clinging to my face. I inhale and feel my body choke, my lungs burn. Maybe Hazel was right. Maybe being on fire, just a little bit, is preferable, a better way to achieve influencer status. I wish I were on fire. I wish I could sear away the rest of me, disappear like ash in the wind.

I curl into bed, toss my phone to the floor. I still have plenty of pills, so I take one. Still in pain. I want to sleep as much as I can.

I wake up to banging at my front door. I forgot to close the window, and there's a haze in the room. I get up, coughing, slide the window shut, and turn on the large circular fan.

"Pet! Petra! Please." It's Hazel.

I throw on a hooded robe, covering as much of myself as possible. I open the door, and she's standing there in her own incognito mode, wearing a loose jumpsuit, flip-flops, a hooded sweater, sunglasses, and a fancy mask printed with skeleton teeth.

We look at each other for a moment, then I pull her into the apartment and walk her over to the couch. I toss a throw blanket over the mini-fridge. We sit down together, not making eye contact.

"Petra, I'm sorry."

"I'm sorry too. I should have talked to you. Consulted with you."

"I was a bad mentor. I didn't warn you about things enough. I only wanted us to have a good time and make money. I'm so sorry."

I reach over and put a hand on her knee, and she puts her hand over mine.

"No, you're a good mentor. I made a mistake." I start to cry, and the tears sting my face. I delicately wipe at my healing skin.

"Listen, I know we're both not doing great right now, like, I'm not even sure what we're gonna do. But I say we just go for it. Use what we've got."

"I just show people this face?"

"Yeah."

"You won't even look at me."

She takes down her hood and motions for me to do the same. I do. She smiles at me.

"Neon made a mistake, and look where she is now. Fuck it."

I think about Neon's endorsements, the burn creams, the KN95 masks, the spot on *Live with Justin Bieber Jr. III & Emma-Jenna-Lea Schwarzenegger-Cruise*. Her world blew open, and now she has to turn down sponsored content because she doesn't even have enough time in the day. While she's healing, she's making money.

"No one's ever had what I have."

"That's right, Pet, that's right." Hazel reaches into her pocket and takes out her phone.

"And we're gonna do this together," I say. "We really are. I'm ready."

And then there we are, together, going live.

In the fluffy change purse inside her zippered wallet bag, there are six toonies. Half of them are for an expired bottle of mocha from the corner store on her way back home. They sell them half price when they're expired. She can spend another two on a new piece of poster board. The last one she'll slip into the chipped coin bowl her mom keeps on the kitchen table. She'll be late for school, but she's only missing gym class. If she ever checked her health app, she'd be over ten thousand steps every day. But measuring steps is bullshit. Her mom walks double that on an average shift at the bistro. After school, she can sharpen her X-Acto knife. There are more flimsy building notices to deface. She's got the time. And she'll keep it up until she's done them all, or she has to leave the city, or the city doesn't even exist.

UNDER MY THUMB

The last person has left my house, and that means I can stop thinking about anything related to funerals. I had already gotten comfortable an hour ago, putting on my slippers and removing my jewellery piece by piece—now it's all over the house. Eventually, I'll find it all and put it back where it belongs. The end of January is such a typical time for a funeral. It was so natural for Len to do things as expected, including dying appropriately.

I wander through the house, looking at things people have left for me and things I should have put away before guests arrived, things I should have been embarrassed by but wasn't. Everyone hugged me properly. That was the best part of today. Not one hug too hard or too soft, no weird side hugs.

I pick up a cake slice and carry it around in my bare hand without a napkin. Someone brought a grief cake, and it was right: "SORRY YOUR HUSBAND IS DEAD" in dark-blue icing. I take a bite of cake and crumbs spill onto the carpet. There's a vacuum for a reason. I poke around the empty rooms to see if I've discarded a ring or a bracelet there. Collecting my discarded jewellery will be a game.

At the back of the hall, I flick on the light in the gym. I haven't been in here in months but might as well check every room, now that I've started. The new stationary bike is almost blocking the door, and the room is so full of equipment it would have been impossible to use anything even if I felt like it. The bike still has a card and bow taped to the handlebars. "To my Sylvia, Happy Birthday! There's always time to get on track! Love, Len." The same sentiment as he wrote in every birthday card to me over the past ten years. Except this one arrived when he was too sick to test the equipment himself. The only machine in the room he didn't use. I turn out the light, shut the door, and crawl upstairs into bed with my cake.

I'm lucky I moved into this house when I did. My husband was a few years away from paying it off. He was older than me and one of those people everyone said was smart with money. What they meant was that he understood how to play the game and could afford to take chances that paid off. But even if you know how to play the game, you can't stave off all the bad things, including kidney failure. And those people were wrong, anyway. He wasn't smart, just lucky that he got the house when he did, that the city hadn't yet become a development hell back then. And unlucky that his body decided he couldn't enjoy his beloved Beaujolais by the bottle daily anymore.

The last couples' dinner we had before he got sick was at his favourite place. Our very old friends Kevin and Brent invited us. Len insisted on picking the restaurant and the time and almost ordered for the table.

"Are you ready to order?" the server asked, hands clasped tightly.

"Why don't we each get different entrees? Then we can all enjoy a bit of each."

"Oh Len, you know I have dietary restrictions. And I've honestly been dying to try the seafood here," Kevin said.

"I'll have the handmade ravioli," I said and handed the menu to the server.

Len looked up from the wine list at me. "Fine, everyone get what you like. But let me pick the wine."

"Of course, Len. Everyone knows you're the wine guy."

We all laughed, Len ordered the wine, and I took a gulp of ice water.

Kevin reached over to touch the sleeve of my tunic, rubbing the fabric between his fingers.

"This is lovely, and you look lovely in it, Sylvia."

"I never know what to wear these days. We should go shopping sometime."

The server brought over the wine and opened it for Len to taste.

"Let me make you something. I love working with people I love."

"You're too good to me. A custom Kevin piece? I'm in!"

Len indicated the wine was acceptable, and the server filled our glasses. Instinctively, we all raised our glasses and said, "Cheers!"

"Too bad Kevin's losing his studio space," Brent said, tipping wine into his mouth.

"What? No."

"They sold the building, and it's so hard to find anything that isn't outrageously priced for a rental that size."

"Can you buy something?" Len asked.

"Buying is even more outrageous than renting. I'll have to work from home for a bit. It'll take getting used to, but there might be opportunities to partner with some other designers and textile artists in a year or so. Brent is doing well at work, and we have our condo.

There are people in way worse situations. So many people can't even afford to rent a small apartment. It's scary out there."

"It's scary for sure. To see what's being built and what's coming down and who's left in the city. Think of all our friends who aren't here anymore," Brent said.

When our meals arrived, we all stopped talking for a while, overwhelmed by how delicious everything was. Nothing but the clamour of the restaurant and our own happy food sounds until Len burst in.

"If they're not smart enough to figure it out, they don't deserve to live here," he said, sliding his knife into the lamb on his plate, juice oozing. I identified with the slab of meat losing juice.

"Who, Len?" Brent asked.

"Everyone who's had to leave. We all earned our place. And they couldn't hack it."

I took a gulp of wine and grabbed the dessert menu.

"Look at what Mitt Johnson's done for our neighbourhood. For the whole city. He's transformed things, he's made health a priority, and he's gotten rich off of it. What a way to excel." Len poured himself yet another glass and sloshed it around.

"The MindfulLegs guy?" Brent asked.

"He's more than his Pilates pants—he's created an empire. And he lives just a few blocks away from us."

"I thought he was cancelled for agreeing with the Dalai Lama about women not being allowed to become the Dalai Lama," Kevin said, winking at me as he took the last bite of his meal.

"Why would anyone care about that? Ridiculous line of conversation. I'm still not even sure what 'cancelled' means," Len said.

"Who wants to think about dessert?" I interjected.

Kevin held his wine up. "I always want to think about dessert."

During the car ride home, Len insisted on driving, even though we had a rule about how many glasses of wine and who drove. I'd had one and he'd had four. More than two and he was supposed to hand over the keys.

"I know the best things on that menu. No one ever wants to listen to me."

"They're just not people to be pushed around at mealtime. They like to eat."

"I like to eat."

"I know, but you only like certain things. Not everyone is like that."

"Not everyone eats only carbs for every meal." He sped up to catch an amber light before it went red. "Carbs are not something a person should constantly be putting into their body, Sylvia."

I stared out the window at the very typical rain, thinking about the warm pockets of doughy pasta I'd enjoyed and knives slicing into flesh.

I was supposed to be a trophy wife. I was younger, but I wasn't a model or trying to be one. Two years in, I wasn't quite young enough, didn't stay hot enough, wasn't fit enough for him. But I wanted to please him, so when he started buying the exercise machines, I thought, *Why not? I barely work, I only volunteer twice a week; I should make this my focus.* But no matter what or how little I ate, how much I exercised, my body didn't change. And I was fine with it, but the machines started to build up in the room. I never went in there. Len would order them, they'd be delivered, he'd place a card on them, and when he came home from work he'd ask if I'd used them, and I'd say I hadn't found the time. Then somehow, thirty years went by, and I was in my fifties and he was in his seventies, and now he's dead.

I'd worked in data entry a floor below Len's. I used to eat in the concrete garden in front of the building, hating to hear my co-workers all chewing at once in the cramped lunchroom. He started to come by and talk to me from another bench, then eventually he migrated to my bench, and then we started kissing and getting frisky in the alley, and six months later, we went on a real date, and a year later we were married. Every week he brought me little gifts: a plant that wouldn't die on my sad desk, magnets for the file cabinet, hemp-heart chocolate. He told me my skin was luminous as he gripped my waist in the crowded elevator. He had a big house, told me I wouldn't have to work if I didn't want to, and he promised to give me whatever I wanted. I wanted to get out of my roommate's way so she could continue to date the most annoying men in Vancouver, and I wanted to cook and be loved and live in a giant house in the fancy part of town. I wanted to be taken care of. I wanted things to be easy.

Our house isn't even big, not compared to ones just a few blocks away, but it's in Kitsilano, close to Point Grey, so the land is expensive. The house is twice my age and hasn't been updated much—three bedrooms, two and a half baths, a den, a double garage. It's worth probably three cents. But the ground it sits on is evaluated at $3 million. We have no kids. "I only want you," he said, and I was relieved. I didn't want to raise anything besides flowers in the corner of the yard. And the weeds that inevitably grew and that I grew to love. Those machines taking up space in the den were the babies. And now it's time to get them out of the house.

The neighbourhood started to get less enjoyable when Mitt, the Pilates mogul, moved in. That wasn't long after I moved into Len's, and this was before he was a mogul. One of the first things he did after his arrival was to start a petition to keep "undesirable" people out of the neighbourhood. He didn't like that sometimes people used the Seawall near his house, so he petitioned to get that part declared private property. People ignored him, the petition was unsuccessful, and the area was still filled with "riff-raff." Then, he started complaining that too many ugly people were spending time on that part of the beach. That also went nowhere, but it didn't matter.

All the while, he was starting up his MindfulLegs clothing line, which became an empire. The same people he wanted to keep out of the square footage interrupting his view would line up to get into his stores' grand openings. They'd get their purchases in a cheap recycled-plastic tote bag emblazoned with meaningless philosophical quotes taken out of context. The words of Ayn Rand next to Dr. Phil's. What did it matter? It was said that he forced employees to go to cultlike self-improvement seminars. Of course, there were accusations of poor labour practices. And the price point on the clothing sold at his thousands of stores went up and up.

Our first encounter was barely memorable. Len recognized him as we were walking home from the salad restaurant. Len didn't care about fashion, but Mitt had been featured in *Vancouver Business Weekly* because he was approaching his first billion. He was wearing tight leggings that hugged his knotty body and standing in what was now a vast front yard with a large gate protecting it all.

Len waved and walked over. "Love what you've done with the place."

I stood behind him on the sidewalk, unsure of what to say to someone who was about to become a billionaire. I looked up and all I could see was the outline of his balls through his Pilates pants. I stared back at the concrete.

"Thank you. I think this neighbourhood needs more privacy. It's so close to non-single-family dwellings, whatever we can do to carve out some space for ourselves feels right."

"Definitely, definitely."

"Yes, we have a lot of work to do if we're going to maintain this beautiful area for ourselves! And I'll be backing whatever needs backing to keep things the way they are, maybe even make them better."

"Congratulations, by the way. From a few pairs of pants to billions. Pilates really pays."

"Yes, it does. Not only monetarily, of course. Though that part has been great for me. But it's an important practice. It reminds me to be aware of myself and my needs."

"That is important. Certainly."

"It's something you can do alone, which is really what drew me to it. Pilates is personal responsibility."

"Well, congratulations on all your success. I'm Len, this is Sylvia." Len stepped aside so Mitt could see me.

"Hello there." Mitt waved at me like I was a child. I didn't return the gesture. "Don't ask me for any discount coupons! I don't have them here. Ha."

"Well, we should be going."

We continued on our way, me walking at a clip, Len following behind, trying to catch up.

By spring, I've sold Len's British sports cars and donated the money to a women's shelter. Every time I sell something of his, I give the money away.

The doorbell rings. Kevin's arrived. And he's been to the good doughnut shop.

"If we're going to be doing physical labour, we need to carbo-load."

"Thanks for helping me. I want to get everything out of the gym room and into the garage."

Kevin goes to the trunk of his vehicle and pulls out a flatbed cart, a dolly, and then another dolly. I don't know what he thinks the two of us will do, but I appreciate his commitment to my needs.

"You really went all out."

"Anything for you. Honestly I just wasn't sure what we'd need. I actually brought three dollies."

I laugh and grab a caramel apple fritter from the doughnut box. The fancy doughnuts smell so sweet and good. He went all out in all ways.

I've been parking my car in the carport, so the double garage is pretty empty. Lots of room to arrange everything. We struggle to get the flatbed dolly up the step into the house. Kevin rides it like a skateboard across the hardwood. I laugh, thinking how Len would have hated to see us scuffing the floor. But I don't care what happens to the hardwood.

We start with the elliptical machine, which just fits on the dolly bed. We wheel it through the narrow hallway, and when we turn it in the entryway, the handles knock a landscape painting off the wall. The glass frame smashes on the ground.

"Shit, sorry. I guess I'm not very good at driving this," Kevin says.

I move to go clean up the mess, but as soon as my hands leave the machine, it tips, so I grip my side of it tightly again.

"Let's not worry about that right now," I say. "Just be careful. Keep your shoes on. We'll get this out first."

"Okay, but I'm helping to sweep it up. And I can get it reframed."

"Honestly, I don't care what happens to it. I don't even like it. It was here before I moved in. Just another interpretation of nature. Eh."

"I like it!"

"Take it, it's yours."

Finally, we get the elliptical into the garage. I've got the floor marked so I can keep track of every piece coming in. They should all fit on one side of the garage. The other side I've outfitted with new tools. Long coils of extension cord sit like neon snakes on the new workbench, and I paid the neighbour's son to install a wall-mounted TV. If I'm going to be spending a lot of time in here, I want to be entertained.

We manage to get everything moved by early afternoon. Both of us are sweating and tired, but I've premade iced tea cocktails. Kevin cleans up the mess, as promised. I tell him to meet me at the iron table under the patio umbrella. I grab the pitcher and two glasses, a bottle of gin just in case, and put everything on a tray along with the rest of the doughnuts.

Outside, the sun is red. The wildfire smoke levels aren't high enough to keep us inside, but they are enough to make me concerned when I catch a glimpse of the sun.

"Thank you for your help."

"Are you kidding me? It feels good to be useful for once. If I can't get a studio space soon, I'm going to have to find a way to get paid to watch *Judge Judy Bot*."

"I'll pay you to watch TV with me."

"Stop it."

"Okay, but how about I buy you a studio?"

"That's ridiculous. No. You're still grieving. Don't spend all your money."

The crows are being noisy in the tree next door. I chug the rest of my iced tea and toss the ice cubes into the tree. The crows go wilder for a moment. I chuckle and pour myself a fresh glass.

"Well then, what if I let you work in the garage? After I finish a project, it'll be all yours. I hope to only need it for a couple of weeks."

Kevin stirs his iced tea with a glass straw and stares at me. His cheeks are pinched.

"It's up to you, Kevin."

He drinks the rest of his first glass, and I pour him another. He's eyeing the gin, so I add a little more to his glass. We'll have to get Brent to come pick him up if we keep this up all afternoon.

"I'm not against it. I've never heard you use the word *project*. Are you struggling? Do you need things to do? I want to know what your project is. Come on."

I stare down into the brown liquid, feeling the gin take hold of my head, making it just foggy enough.

"I don't think I'm ready to talk about it. But I'm ready for something more than doughnuts."

I go back to the kitchen and fill a second pitcher with water. In the fridge, I've prepared a board of meats, cheeses, fruits, olives. I place two small plates and forks on the tray and snag a sleeve of crackers that cost as much as a fancy cocktail and a demi-baguette under my arm. Last, I pull a knife from the block and set it over top of everything on the board. Walking back to the deck, I can feel everything starting to slip, so I drop into a squat and lean back. Everything shifts toward me. The knife blade slowly slides between my clavicles. Kevin jumps up from his seat and gently pulls it away from me. I put down the tray and reach up to touch my neck. There's no blood on my fingertips.

"Shit, you're giving me a million scares today."

"I'll be fine. I really will. I feel just fine." I refill our glasses. "Cheers!"

We clink.

"You're freaking me out, but I think I like it."

"Come back next week and check on me. See where I'm at."

I've added pot lights, so the garage is brightly lit. Where the sports cars used to live, there's now a small workstation that's working out all right.

Before I go to sleep, I watch EverEverStream videos on how to hack exercise equipment. Watch tattooed cutie pies unscrew and unlatch and unhitch and remove. It's so much easier to follow in video format. I think of the IKEA instructions me and my boy-wild roommate tried to interpret into the night all those years ago. Then I watch these smart young people repurposing pieces, so resourceful. Elliptical bikes, all-in-ones, rowing machines. I fall asleep feeling impressed with their ingenuity.

Every morning I get up at 6 a.m. and make a large pot of coffee, then prepare French toast or pancakes with fruit and yogurt and sausage. Len preferred bacon, but I always felt it was too salty, and I never liked the crispiness. I have one cup of coffee with breakfast and add the rest to a carafe, then I head into the garage, fire up the lights, turn on the TV, and put on my work gloves.

I spent the first few mornings taking apart the bikes, keeping the mechanical wheels in a small pile beside the workbench. I have my laptop nearby in case I need to rewatch and review videos. Today I'm working on the elliptical. The bars are harder to remove than the young ones led me to believe. I try six different screwdrivers and three wrenches before I make any progress. Once I've got them off I line them up, each one propped across two sawhorses. Right now, I'm trying to get the shape right. I want to do what I was taught in the videos: measure twice, cut once. But in this case, I want to detach slowly and remove carefully and reattach once. Once I've fused things together, it's going to be a lot harder to change the structure.

I focus on learning and disassembling that first week, Monday to Friday. My first nine-to-five since my early twenties. I'm exhausted, but it actually feels good to have a purpose, even if it seems frivolous so far.

When I'm done for the day, I toss my clothes in the laundry room and shower in the tiny guest bathroom. Draped in the silk robe Len got me this past Christmas, I reheat stew on the stove, warm bread in the oven. I love my range. I love this oven. It cost as much as a car and works like a dream. Everything in the kitchen was replaced a few years ago, because I insisted. It was the first time I'd really asked for anything. The old oven wouldn't heat properly anymore.

"I need to be able to bake. For my mental health," I'd said.

Len had stared at me. He was eating the disastrous result of my last attempt at a pie. It was gloopy and horrible, I could see it on his face.

"Fine. A good kitchen is a good investment."

I crawl into bed with my dinner and my laptop. The house creaks around me.

Len cared a lot about real estate. One night I was lying awake, hoping he might touch me, but when he didn't, instead I envisioned his dreams. His face was rubbery and relaxed, his lips forming a dopey grin. He must be thinking of selling our house, the market being what it was right now. In his ear, I whispered softly, "I hope the bubble bursts."

The next morning, I didn't make coffee. Instead, I took myself on a long walk along Point Grey Road. Mitt's giant house was at the end of the last block. He'd been on the news a lot lately, having just sold his most profitable company, the one that made women feel like they had to wear tight leggings to exercise in order to fit a smaller size of those same leggings.

Just a week before, sitting down to watch TV after dinner, I'd flipped to *Entertainment News Network*, and there he was, standing in front of his first store, once a tiny storefront and now a flagship behemoth.

Interviewer: You've made athleisure into an industry, a billion-dollar business!

Mitt: Well, you know, people yearn for relaxation but also perfection. I just saw what people wanted, and I made them want it more. To be healthy, beautiful, and in peak condition.

Interviewer: Recently you were asked about expanding the size range of your line of clothing. What do you have to say to that?

Mitt: I think our clothes should be aspirational. They don't look good on larger bodies, and if people want to wear them they have to work for it. Strive! That's our motto. Strive to thrive. Some losses are worth it.

Interviewer: And I hear you're getting into politics. Is that true, Mitt?

Mitt: Well, the best way to make change is to put money where it can do the work. Aspirational!

It was a thirty-minute special devoted to him, his career highlights, even a short tour of his house. Strange that we lived within walking distance of this man.

When Len walked in with a half-finished bottle of wine and sat next to me, he scoffed.

"What is this trash?"

"Yes, he is trash."

"Excuse me! I meant this entertainment show."

He poured himself a glass. There wasn't one for me.

"It's a special about the Pilates mogul. Selling his business. Being a jackass."

He looked at me sternly and took a sip. I jumped off the couch, startling him so that he spilled the red all down his front and onto the carpet.

"What is wrong with you?"

I kicked an errant couch cushion out the open sliding glass door.

"You know what's wrong with me! I don't want any of this stuff you're giving me. I don't want to exercise. I don't want a home gym. I want you to love me and listen to me."

"Calm down. I'm sorry you don't like rich people. But we're well-off people ourselves. I don't know what this man's ever done to you."

"I do not give a fuck about a billionaire mogul who criticizes women's asses for a living. I don't give a rat's ass what happens to him. I care about what you think of me."

He huffed and went into the bathroom, locking the door. I slumped back down on the couch and drained the rest of his precious wine straight from the bottle. I lay on the floor and flipped through channels, stopping to watch a dating show where contestants got married after texting each other only emojis for a week, *Emoji Marriage*. Len came back in and sat on the couch in his same old spot.

"You're mean to me, Syl."

I sighed, pulled my knees into my body, and pushed my face into the fabric of my leggings, the kind made to properly fit a body like mine, not some aspirational pants. I rolled over. Stayed like that until he stopped talking, got up, turned off the television and the lights, and went to bed.

The last machine, the NordicTrack Fusion, is a breeze to take apart, but each piece is so specific to that beast of all-in-one machinery that finding a place for them all is proving difficult. It isn't made of metal but some indestructible synthetic material. And every piece is connected with small, thick circles of rubber. My intent is to use the Nordic's smaller and more durable inner bits to create some movement in the final piece. But every time I remove something, the tinier bits seem more and more useless. It requires cutting off each rubber piece too, which is time-consuming, because I'm trying to salvage as much as I can.

By the time I've pulled the whole thing apart, I'm standing in a mess of the strangest, smallest, and most useless pieces of plastic I've ever seen in my life, with a small pile of dusty rubber bits that I can't even reuse. I pile them up on the workbench, and they stare back at me like fifty tiny evil eyes.

From the mounted tool wall, I take an axe and attack the drive belt. Bits of rubber fly everywhere. I chop and chop and chop and chop and then the axe flies out of my hand and hits the inside of the garage door. I envision it ricocheting back and cracking me in the forehead, but it merely drops to the ground with a small thud.

I sit down on the floor, panting, lean over to pick up one of the moulded pieces from the front and stare into the silvery logo. I start crying and bash the piece into my face. It's so heavy I hear my nose crunch. It's hard. These large pieces are several feet long. And sturdy. They're what I need. Not these tiny bits. I gather the other big pieces, clutch them to my chest, and continue crying with relief.

🔥

When he said he was leaving me later that week, I knew it was only in part because he wasn't interested in me anymore and because he thought I was mean to him and mostly because his interest was elsewhere. He was interested in the redevelopment signs and the friendship he'd started with Mitt. They'd recently done golf Pilates together and had made plans to do paddleboard goat yoga together too.

Then he got sick. I stayed by his side. Because what else do you do? No one else knew what he'd said to me, and he got sick so quickly that he didn't have time to announce it to his friends and colleagues. His eyes glazed over every time I spoke. But I cooked, I drove him to appointments, I took the bus all the way to the other side of town when the car broke down and he needed special slippers that very day. When someone close to you is sick, even someone you've come to think of as an asshole, you take care of them. You know they aren't the very worst and don't deserve to be abandoned. Even though part of you wants to blast them through the roof with a firehose.

Back when we first met, he made it seem like I wouldn't ever have to worry. Which felt like a relief, for a while. A safety net even if I had to be uncomfortable some of the time. Worry finds a person, though. I didn't have to worry about money. That part was true.

🔥

The blowtorch and soldering iron were delivered yesterday afternoon, and like a kid on Christmas Eve, I barely slept the night before. I didn't use them yesterday because I wanted to be well rested before playing with new toys. I'd watched videos and tried to practise the techniques using the clothes steamer. I looked like I was aggressively trying to get wrinkles out of a blazer.

I slice open the top of the package with a box cutter and pull out the blowtorch. It's smaller than I expected, but I chose the sage-green model, and it's gorgeous. Simple, just add butane. I could fit it in my purse and whip it out if anyone needs something fixing. "Oh this? It's just my blowtorch, no big deal."

The soldering iron is more complicated. It requires a bit more practice and will be useful for precision work. Though thankfully it came in a similar colour. Like outfitting the kitchen with matching appliances, I am making my tool wall as aesthetically coordinated as possible.

I've saved a pile of small discarded pieces to use as practice material. I put on the welder's mask and heat-resistant gloves, also light green, and start with the blowtorch. I blast it too hot at first, and terrified of the intensity, I drop the too-small piece of rowing machine I've selected. Even with the protective equipment, I feel my face flush like I'm doubling up on menopausal hot flashes. I turn down the BTU slightly, grab a larger scrap metal tube. I hold the torch too close this time, and the metal melts quickly. Next I find two pieces about a foot long each and set them in a X shape. I steady my hand, hold the blowtorch a little farther away, and keep the butane flowing, but not too much. One of the metal pieces bends to the curve of the other. I grab another piece and do the same thing again, adding more odds and ends, all the while maintaining focus, careful to not lock my arm.

"Holy shit!"

Kevin's standing in the side door, the door open wide behind him. He's cackling.

I turn off the blowtorch and put down the metal pieces, pushing them away and trying to hide them under a tarp we never used for the firewood we never bought before we replaced the wood-burning fireplace with a gas one.

"Kevin. I didn't know you were coming by."

"I haven't heard from you in weeks. I was worried about you and wanted to check how you're doing. And, shit, you really are doing something." I flip up my mask and take off my gloves. "Really, though. Are you okay?"

"I'm better than okay. I'm doing what I really want to be doing."

I look around the garage, try to see what Kevin sees. A bunch of random junk thrown around, a mess, the disarray of the dismembered high-end exercise equipment that had once cost hundreds of thousands of dollars. I scramble to pick up some stray bits, toss my gloves and mask to the floor, and walk him out the way he came in, flicking off the light and closing the door. Outside, we're pelted with rain. Kevin opens his umbrella but I don't even get under it.

"Are you okay?" he asks again, pulling me under the umbrella with him.

I grab his hand and lead us to the front door. Once we're inside I just stare at him, dripping water onto the hardwood floor. My cheeks are flushed. I don't know if it's from the heat of welding or from embarrassment.

"Honestly, I don't want to talk about it. I don't want to talk about anything. I just want to do my own thing that I want to do."

Kevin puts his wet umbrella in the holder. I take off my shoes. We go into the kitchen.

"Okay, fine. You don't have to tell me, but be safe, I guess. If I'm not good enough to know, then I'm not good enough to know."

I pour us two glasses of water, chug mine, refill it, and drink it down.

"It's not about you. I'm trying out a new phase in my life, and I want to make sure I can do it. Finish my own project on my own terms."

"Are we only drinking water?"

I get some wine from the fridge and pour some for us both.

"I can't tell you because you'll be incriminated. So don't ask. Just know that the place is all yours for art-based uses once I'm done in there. I've even had extra keys made for you. For the garage and the whole house. I've got the security code for you and everything."

"What? Thank you."

"I meant to have you over or something to tell you all this, but I've been busy doing my own thing. I'm sorry."

"I already feel left out of everything because I don't have a space to work anymore. I never really see anyone. Except you, and I haven't seen you in ages."

While he's talking, I assemble salty snack bowls. Nuts, chips, cheese straws. The last time I saw him, he helped me to move everything, and we had such a good day.

"I'm sorry. I know I need to be better and to see people. Maybe being alone is part of my grieving process."

"Is playing with fire part of your grieving process?"

"No talking about that. And yes, it obviously is."

I see Mitt on the news, this time being interviewed about an organization he funds and the donations he's made to a right-wing mayoral candidate who wants to bulldoze the poor neighbourhoods.

> Interviewer: You're backing a candidate who has his sights set on the development of some lower-income areas. This candidate has ties to real estate developers, including the largest, Platinum Corp.
>
> Mitt: I am merely funding a non-profit organization that supports the work he'll be doing. I think that ensuring every area of the city is at its best is important to everyone. Some buildings with mould, bedbugs, improper plumbing, they need to go. And we've seen

the work Platinum Corp has done to clean up so many areas. Including their beautiful community garden initiatives.

Interviewer: So you support Platinum Corp? Are they not gentrifiers?

Mitt: That word feels like a slur. We have stores in several Platinum Corp buildings in the city, and they are excellent caretakers.

Interviewer: Also, there are reports that the Proud Boys and similar groups are inspired by your work. I've even heard that some of them are getting into Pilates!

Mitt: Well, if I can get anyone to care more about their health and physical appearance, I'm proud of myself. Aspirational!

Late on Friday night, I put on the finishing touches. Add a little paint, smooth some of the edges, solder a few spots that seem like they might not be sturdy. The wheels are clunky but functional—the elliptical rollers actually make it roll more smoothly than if I'd just used the hard wheels from inside the bikes. The NordicTrack bits make the base more durable, and the seat from the original bike is cushioned and comfortable.

Before turning in for the night, I call Kevin.

"Thought I might catch you tonight for a bottle of wine. Last minute, I know. Anyway, let me know when you want to start using the garage space. It's got Wi-Fi, a TV, electricity, everything you need. A workbench. But it's yours. I'm done with it. Love you."

The TV's tuned to the local news broadcast. Wildfire season continues. A celebrity filming in town is accused of sexually assaulting seven crew members. There's another protest at the site of a development just up the hill from here. I turn up the volume. Watch my neighbours gathered onscreen. Platinum Corp is trying to displace even more people, who are running out of places to go and speak their minds. How anyone manages to still live here is a miracle. No, it's resilience. Along with Platinum Corp, the development belongs to none other than the athleisure mogul himself. A marriage of conglomerates. They're turning out an entire block of small businesses that can barely afford the current rent. They'll be adding in high-priced retail with state-of-the-art condos on top. Video of Mitt Johnson comes on. It's a statement made from his private island and posted on his social media to share with the protesters.

> Thank you for your concerns about our city. I once was a small business owner, and look at me now. Failure builds character, and character builds a better business. I'll also be offering $5,000 mural sponsorships to ten artists who will temporarily decorate the areas around this new retail–housing space. I want to be able to give back and share beauty with those who live there. By revitalizing these areas, we'll be able to generate more income for more people. And isn't that what we all want? Don't forget to register for the PilatesTakes the Park community shutdown of the streets near the park. All the money will be going to help fund these artists as they help beautify this community. Let's stay healthy, stay fit, and stay together. Be well!

I shut off the TV and put on my raincoat, slip into my rubber boots, and grab my wallet. The rain is unrelenting, but I jog to the protest, hoping it's still happening and that I wasn't watching an older clip.

The protesters' signs are clever and cute: "Keep Your Shitty Condos!" "Occupy Shaughnessy! Occupy Point Grey! Occupy Mitt Johnson's House!" "We Can't Live in Your Leggings Because You Don't Make Them Big Enough!" Mitt Johnson's face is plastered on many of them, defaced with a line through a circle, a Mr. Yuk Poison Help! sticker, *X*'s for eyes. I picture the selfie my dead husband texted me of that same man's face right beside his own. He wasn't very good at selfies, but somehow the light was right, and they looked like old buddies. I feel oddly wistful, knowing he was so happy to send me a photo with a famous stranger. The text read, "Neighbours! 😛" I choke on a sob. Memories are strange.

Hood pulled tight around my face, I feel like I'm merely a pair of eyes. There are hundreds of people here. Between the chants of the protesters, I hear snippets of conversations as I weave in and out of the crowd. Someone in a thin denim jacket was just renovicted. A couple with twins tell a friend they're going to the food bank every week. A small man in a wheelchair whispers to his companion with a mutt in a raincoat that more housing advocates are missing today. A teen rattles a can of spray paint and touches up a sign that reads "RENOVICT MY ASS."

There's a counter-protest across the street, about fifteen people standing on the corner with their own signs. Less clever, less cute. "Protect Our Houses!" Not catchy.

"Our properties are in danger!" they shout.

"In danger of what? Being worth even more money?" I mutter.

The person next to me chuckles, and I smile at her. "Who organized this?" I ask. The person next to her replies.

"Affordable Homes Now. It's a small group. We're on social media and have a website. Look us up."

"I will, thank you."

"You live around here?"

"I do. My name's Sylvia."

"Me too, for now I live around here. Nice to meet you, Sylvia."

For a while I watch both protests, the large group stopping traffic in the street and the small crowd huddled together on the sidewalk. A woman in the smaller crowd who looks vaguely familiar seems to wave me over. I don't wave back. She raises her hand and shouts something, possibly my name, but the chanting from the housing group protest drowns her out. Then I remember that the woman was on some committee Len insisted I join to do something with my life, like other wives did. This one was to beautify alleys. I told them that natural wildflowers and flowering weeds would easily crop up on their own, but they weren't interested. They wanted finicky flowers, delicate peonies. I went to the one meeting and never went back.

The woman wants me to join the counter-protestors. She thinks I'm like them. I can hear them shouting, trying to convince anyone to join their side.

"There are way more people on their side!"

"It's unfair!"

"We've lived here longer! Who do they think they are?"

It doesn't matter what they think of me, and I don't care about them. I take the long way back, curling up a side street and through an alley to make it back around to the quiet street blocked off to commoners. I see Mitt Johnson's house, looming. My street is on the other side. I start to run, passing houses as big as Mitt's and some smaller, all of them adorned with non-native flowers and trees that are immaculately pruned. If they're not, someone will drop a nasty note on the owners' doorstep. The westernmost part of the city is still populated with single-family homes, some of the most expensive real estate in North America, but every day I feel more divided from those next door and down the block, pulled away from my neighbours.

According to his social media, Mitt's on some spiritual quest in India. He's staying in a fancy hotel designed to look like a hut. Poverty tourism. His wife is launching a Pilates mat bag line in Germany.

At home, I nap until it's dark out and then wait until after midnight. Then I get up, click the garage-door opener, and excitedly jog in place while waiting for it to open. I grab my work gloves, a pack of matches, and jump into the beast. I secure my bike helmet on my head. The vehicle is open on both sides, without doors, so I'm glad I don't have to go very far. I start it up, and it rumbles to life. The machine is clunky, but it drives. It moves. I can turn around in the now-empty garage, though I'm not sure whether it'll go much farther. The engine I bought off an old guy on the local online marketplace was for a moped. I grab the blowtorch from the work table and set it across my lap.

The front is adorned with clickable bike lights, like blinking eyes. I'd envisioned something like Godzilla, but there was no way I could make something with that much height. This looks more like a mechanical mosquito, but with a battering ram constructed out of two dozen metal handles, and twenty-kilogram weights from the leg press instead of a needlelike proboscis.

I pull out into the street and try not to steer into the luxury cars parked along both sides. The front end is so long I have to do a seven-point turn to get it facing the right direction. Every movement jerks me around. I should have added a seat belt. When I make it to the corner, I cheer for myself. Then I turn into the alley. I keep my speed low. I'm only two blocks away.

At the end of the block, I try not to crash through the rhododendrons, which are so perfect this time of year, resilient and fragrant. But I can't steer as well I'd hoped, and it's a tight squeeze. I scrape the side of a BMW parked under the bush, back up, and right myself. Every move feels like it's taking ten years. It's still quiet out. I hope no one is filming this.

Finally, I see Mitt's house. The gate is closed, as usual. I rev the engine to try to get as much momentum as I can. Then I speed forward, bashing the front end into the gate. It doesn't budge, but I can feel something drop off the back end of the machine and crash to the ground. I back up again and ram. This time things hold. I back up again and ram. Back up. Ram. Back up. Ram. Back up. Ram. And then the whole gate bursts open. The alarm that immediately sounds is piercing.

But I keep going. I drive overtop of his front yard putting green, leaving treads in my wake. I swerve into the flower bed, leaning out one side to grab at plants with my bare hand. The back end catches a shrub and uproots it. I'm dragging bushes through the Zen garden. The machine is tough to manoeuvre over the concrete enclosure, but I make it up onto the geometric fountain. There's no water in it, but in the centre is a sculpture of a woman wearing cropped Pilates pants, bent over. I rev, back up, and ram, back up and ram, back up and ram into her toned rock ass until it topples over. Security lights are swirling in the air, the screech of the alarm unrelenting. Backing out of the fountain, now I turn and drive straight up the two steps to the front door.

I only have to ram three times before the wood splinters and the lock slides to the ground. And once the door is open, I go straight through. The alarm reverberates through the plastic of my helmet. The entryway is grey and sad. There are photos of Mitt all along the stairway. No family portraits. A classic image of him stern-faced in a gold frame, except instead of a suit he's wearing a shirt made of sweat-wicking fabric. Across from that, several faux Warhols of his face in a quad. A full-body portrait of him topless on a fainting couch, like George Costanza. And a replica of *American Gothic* with him in both roles, a bag of money instead of a rake, and instead of a farmhouse there's a factory churning Pilates pants out of its smokestack. It's nauseating and hilarious.

I get out, but the machine won't stop moving. I hadn't thought of how to park this thing. It runs forward and almost into me, so I jump back in and try to slow it down as much as I can. There's a large white brick, supposedly art, displayed on a pedestal beside the staircase.

I grab it as I drive by and turn the machine back around so it's facing the rest of the main floor. I crank the speed, set the brick on the gas pedal, and jump out the side, blowtorch in hand. To the right of the broken door is a human-sized candle in Mitt's image. I fire up the blowtorch and light the wick.

The vehicle side-swipes a geometric crystal side table, which shatters, then it bumps over a rug worth more than my whole life and breaks straight through a set of glass doors and into a dining table, which snaps, sending an enormous potted lily crashing to the floor. It keeps going farther into the house, little bits of it breaking off with every little smash, knocking over lamps, shelves, and art as it drives away.

I walk back outside, climb over the back gate, and drop down onto the Seawall. The ocean smells perfect. I circle back down the alley. In my capri pants and silk tunic and expensive running shoes, I look like every other housewife on the block. My neighbours are standing outside in their pyjamas, confused, groggy at 1 a.m. I turn around too, pretending to be a lookie-loo like them, exchange concerned glances. Then I walk home.

I shower, drop my clothes in the washer, and crawl into bed to watch Mitt's house burning from my window. The smoke mixes with the wildfires, and the moon is blood red.

ACKNOWLEDGMENTS

Thank you to Daniel Zomparelli for reading the early and worst drafts of this book and still being willing to read the later drafts and to give me his special and keen eye.

Thank you to Meghan Waitt, who always sees the potential and sends me the notes I need.

Thank you to Jen Sookfong Lee for early encouragement and her editorial excellence when I wasn't sure I was gonna finish this book.

Thank you to Cynara Geissler for coming in clutch and noticing the details I miss and pulling it together like one of her well-curated outfits.

Thank you to Don English for being the best reader I know and for his kind and helpful notes.

You are all such generous readers, and I love you.

Ten million thank yous to my wonderful agent, Kelvin Kong, who helped me shape this book before it went out into the world and who is just a real delight. What an advocate for writers and their work.

Kind of obsessed with Catharine Chen for seeing this book for what it was and could be and for being the kind of editor who makes great things happen. Thank you.

Huge thanks to everyone at Arsenal Pulp Press: again to Cynara (my friend, my love, best publicist in the universe), Brian Lam, Erin Chan, JC Cham, and Robert Ballyntyne made this experience a real nice time. Super thanks to Jazmin Welch who worked on making the perfect cover. It was a joy to work with you.

Thank you to Jeff Dupuis and A.G. Pasquella and Dundurn Press for publishing "I Want Candy" in *Devouring Tomorrow*.

And, for the first time ever, I want to thank the Canada Council for the Arts for awarding me a grant, which I did use to work on this book but also to pay off my students loans from oh so long ago. That really helped me not feel as insane and in debt while I wrote this book.

DINA DEL BUCCHIA is the author of five collections of poetry, *Coping with Emotions and Otters*; *Rom Com*, written with Daniel Zomparelli; *It's a Big Deal!*; and *You're Gonna Love This* (all by Talonbooks); and *Blind Items* (Insomniac Press). For ten years she co-hosted *Can't Lit*, a podcast on Canadian literature and culture, with Jen Sookfong Lee. Her first collection of short stories, *Don't Tell Me What to Do*, was published in 2017 by Arsenal Pulp Press. She was the artistic director of the Real Vancouver Writers' Series and is on the editorial board of fine press. She lives in Vancouver, BC. ***dinadelbucchia.com***